I0817806

CHAMPLAIN STREET

CHAMPLAIN STREET

THE BATTLE OF CHESTNUT HILL

VICTORIA ARENDT

ELUSIVE ORAO

COPYRIGHT

This is a work of historical fiction. Apart from the well-known actual people, events and locales that figure in the narrative, all names, characters, places, and incidents are products of the author's imagination or are used fictitiously.

Published 2022

ISBN 978-1-7346331-8-4 (hardcover) | ISBN 978-1-7346331-1-5 (paperback) | ISBN 978-1-7346331-0-8 (ebook)

Cover design by Lance Buckley Designs

Cover photograph reproduced from author's personal collection

Editing by Raymond Blackburn

Map illustration by Pamela Arendt

Photographs reproduced from author's personal collection

Library of Congress Cataloging-in-Publication Data Name: Arendt, Victoria Title: Champlain Street: The Battle of Chestnut Hill | Victoria Arendt p. cm. Description: Sarasota: Elusive Orao, 2022 Identifiers: LCCN: 2022906911 | ISBN 978-1-7346331-8-4 (hardcover) | ISBN 978-1-7346331-1-5 (paperback) | ISBN 978-1-7346331-0-8 (ebook)

Published by Elusive Orao | www.ElusiveOrao.com | Sarasota, Florida

Printed and bound in the United States of America

For Mary and John

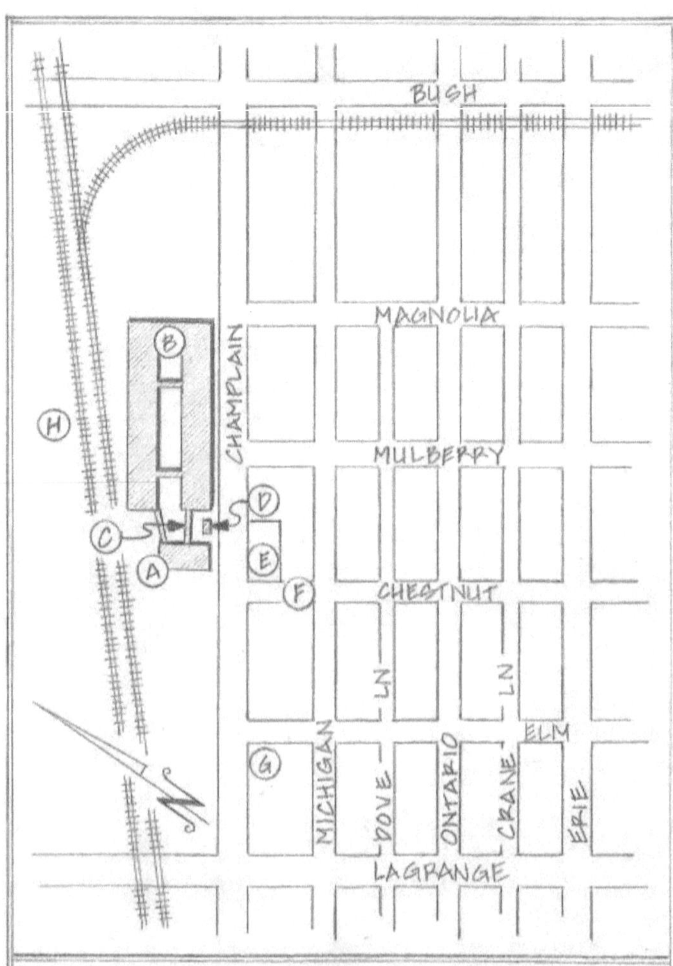

AUTO-LITE STRIKE ZONE

TOLEDO, OHIO · 1934

LEGEND:

A · OFFICE BUILDING
B · FACTORY
C · COVERED WALKWAY
D · GUARD SHACK
E · PARKING LOT
F · CHESTNUT HILL
G · KOOLMOTOR
H · RAILROAD YARD

FOREWORD

The roots of the American labor movement are deeply embedded in the industrial loam of Toledo. Of this fact, Toledoans should take pride, as this was a pivotal moment in an American story that grew from the seeds of discontent, and watered by the blood, and sweat of the working class. As John Steinbeck wrote in the novel "In Dubious Battle", "from these seeds something good is going to grow and that makes it all worthwhile". And so it was that workers, like those at Toledo's giant Auto-Lite plant and other automotive factories, found the audacity to stand up to a system they saw as unfair and unjust in an effort to change it. In doing so, they put their personal security aside and took the risk that they might lose their livelihoods, or lose their lives. And some did.

But in the end, they changed the face of American labor. And that makes it all worthwhile.

As a long-time local reporter and history enthusiast, I've come to appreciate the significance of the events that took place at the Auto-Lite plant on Champlain Street during the Spring of 1934. There is no overstating its importance as to how it helped nurture the growth of the American labor movement. It was a key catalyst that helped spark a larger movement throughout the nation. But beyond the bold headlines of the strike and the violence that rocked our city, lay a deeper story. One that has rarely been told. Perhaps only over a round of beers in a north Toledo saloon, or the kitchen tables in the homes of those who came face to face with the National Guardsmen at Chestnut Hill. From the mouths and memories of those rugged souls who tasted the bitterness of the strike, this was a personal and visceral experience. It is not the headline writer's story. It is their story. One that played out in the theater of human determination and plain old grit. From the seats of power to the streets of unrest, where soldiers in uniform and soldiers of solidarity met on the battlefield of bricks, a tale of struggle and tumult, and eventually, victory. A story that may perhaps be best told by the novel writers who can shape the human contours of what really took place in the hearts and minds of those involved. I am pleased to know that storyteller Victoria Arendt has taken on this task to rekindle these human facets of the famous Auto-Lite strike story. In her new novel "Champlain Street", as she has done before in her book, "Broken Pencils" that examined the past horrors at Toledo's infamous State Hospital, she ably places our understanding of the events of 1934 into the context and comfort of the personal human narrative. A story line that helps one fully appreciate not just this incredible story of courage and change, but of the many Toledo workers, past and future, who would themselves be changed by it. And that makes it all worthwhile.

Lou Hebert
Author and Historian

PART I

Although it is true that only about 20 percent of American workers are in unions, that 20 percent sets the standards across the board in salaries, benefits and working conditions. If you are making a decent salary in a non-union company, you owe that to the unions. One thing that corporations do not do is give out money out of the goodness of their hearts.
~ Molly Ivins

1

CASPER

Casper sat on the factory bench. Sitting down should relax his body, but he was tense. He rotated his head. First in one direction, then the other, releasing tightness that radiated from his neck to his shoulders. He had been sitting on the bench the entire morning, along with the other men of Department Two, waiting to work.

The Toledo manufacturing plant was like most factories in the industrious city: productive, fast-moving and dangerous. He looked around the expansive room. The punch press machines were enormous, soaring to the factory ceiling and dominating the huge space with their presence. Each man working the mammoth machines was keeping time with a steady flow of mechanized force.

Listening to constant, rhythmic, clanging of metal, he slowly leaned forward and let out a sigh. Hunger growled in his stomach.

Glancing at the clock, he recalled last night's supper and fight between his neighbors. It had been over a chicken and who was going to finally eat a decent meal. It was 1934, another tough year, and no one had any money for food.

After much debate, a decision was made and the chicken was split six ways.

His mouth watered.

Lockers were on the other side of the room and his had a deadbolt. He thought of the lunch box inside and the meager piece of salami hidden between thin slices of bread. Stretching his legs, he let his feet slide forward, absorbing the floor's vibration.

"Ring out!" a foreman yelled.

His head snapped up. The locomotive actions of the worker at a punch press stopped. A set-up man was removing a production card, making notations and adding a new one to the machine.

"You!" the foreman yelled. Casper looked at the foreman's extended finger. But, it wasn't pointing at him. He wanted to shake his head and protest, but remembered where that got him last time.

"Ring in," the foreman yelled. "Now!"

Hank, Hank the Hoof, the only man able to make Sixty B's last week, stood up. The long bench bounced from his quick movements, jostling Casper and the row of men. He watched as Hank promptly rang in, documenting his start time, and positioned himself in front of the exposed mechanical giant. It was whirling and rumbling and humming, waiting for a piece of metal.

"I better ring in today," a man's voice said. "I haven't worked all week."

Casper looked at Joe, the worker sitting next to him. He knew all the punch press operators in the department. They were all friends, and they looked out for one another. But, he also knew they were hungry, like him, with mortgages and families to feed. Then he looked at Joe's hands. They were dirty and bruised and scarred, like all the men there, and missing a finger. His own hands were dirty and bruised and scarred, too. But, he had all his fingers *and* his thumbs.

"I don't think The Hoof's gonna make the Sixty B's this week," Joe said. "And, he better be careful with that die, it's pretty tricky."

Casper nodded. He wanted one of the men to make the quota and he wanted that man to be him. But they raised the numbers again and the faster you moved, the more room for error, like being sent home for busting a die. Or worse.

Reclining into the warm bench, he eyed the factory floor. It spanned over one city block and an endless row of long windows covered the walls allowing ample sunlight to shine through. The bench backed up to the windows, but the space was anything but cheerful.

"Ya gotta hand it to him," Joe said. "He sure is trying."

He looked at Hank. He was sweaty, but rigid, quickly pulling a metal sheet from a nearby stack and placing it on an unprotected press plate. The violent machine thrust down, punching iron against metal and as quickly as the punch came down, it ferociously came up. Hank grabbed the altered piece and added it to a growing pile that was stacked to his waist and began the process again.

There wasn't any room for error. Casper knew it. Not even a fraction. And, like Joe said, that particular die was tricky. The punch press left nothing behind and you either kept up with production, or you didn't. And the foreman, well, you better hope he was in a good mood. And that was never. Anything you said or did could get you fired. You just didn't know what that *anything* was.

2

EDITH

EDITH LOOKED at the paper on her desk. The page was filled with a list of names and addresses in her boss's handwriting. Her fingertips hovered over her typewriter and with a push from her left pinky, the shift key moved downward. The letter H was pressed next and a man's name was banged out. She whizzed the carriage return to the next line and the rhythmic clicking continued. An address soon appeared on an index card. Eyeing her flawless work, she removed the card and placed it on a completed stack.

The secretaries' office was quiet except for her workmate, talking into the telephone.

"Yes, sir," Genevieve said. "I'll be right in."

With a flick of her finger, Edith pulled the typewriter bail forward and placed a blank card against the roller.

"That Mr. Miniger," Genevieve said. "He's such an old sweetheart."

Edith paused over the keys as she looked at her workmate. A lacy white collar peeked out over an impeccable black suit, the type of clothing Edith hoped to own someday.

"I'll be right back," Genevieve said. In a few graceful strides, the woman was out the door.

The secretaries' office was located on the top floor in the Electric Auto-Lite office building, a corner space in a three-story structure. It had three desks, three file cabinets, and three large lockers. The room was usually filled with the clicking of typewriters and the two other secretaries, but, at the moment, Edith was alone.

She was surprised on her first day in March, a month ago, when they gave her a desk by a window. It overlooked Champlain Street and the sleepy neighborhood below. Doris, one of the secretaries, told her that although the view was nice, the summertime's open windows would be a distraction. The whistle blowing and changing of the late afternoon factory shift always brought a steady flow of traffic to the corner of Champlain and Chestnut streets. But, Edith loved the view. A spattering of budding tree tops, sprinkled between roofs and tiny yards, made the street look like a pretty pattern. Of course, there was the parking lot on the other side of Champlain, lined with a row of billboards across from the factory building. But, that also looked like a pretty pattern. Especially during the early shift, when methodically parked automobiles formed shiny rows of gray.

She walked over to the window and pulled the curtains open. The warm glow of the room transformed. Eyeing the glass mullions, she looked through one of the panes that made the neighborhood appear wavy and dreamlike. Swaying treetops and meandering chimney smoke lulled her into a daydream until the sudden sound of Genevieve's footsteps brought her attention back into the room.

"Your suit is lovely," Edith said.

"Oh, this old thing?" Genevieve laughed. "It's new. Just got it at Stein's Basement. You should go there."

Edith felt beholden to Auto-Lite and grateful for her job,

especially since most people were unemployed. But, her wages went straight to her grandparent's mortgage. Her wardrobe, which consisted of a few stylish dresses and suits, would have to wait to be expanded. For now, she would wear a different scarf and hat to change her outfit.

"I adore *that* blouse," Genevieve said.

Edith followed the gaze of her workmate, straight to the framed photograph on her desk. "I hope it's okay that I brought in a picture," she said. "It's of my grandmother."

"Of course," Genevieve replied. "Everyone here has a picture of *someone*. Besides, we're *all* family here."

3

CASPER

"Son of a bitch!" the foreman yelled.

The usual factory noises had an added sound, like a surging engine crushing a gear tooth into the wrong sized cog. Casper scanned the room and spotted a stopped punch press. The man working the machine was stiff and motionless, holding a metal sheet as if frozen in ice. But he wasn't in ice.

"You busted the die!" the foreman barked. "Ring out! You're fired."

4

VERN

VERN WAITED IN THE CROWD. The chilly April morning made standing close to others bearable, but he was still cold. A red brick factory stood in front of him and each of its four stories had long rows of large windows. The building extended more than one block on Champlain Street and when he looked down the road, the structure seemed like a lengthy triangle. He reached inside his coat pocket, grabbing a cold, stiff card. The expiration date of his hiring pass was next month and at the rate the two guards were letting in new hires, he would have to apply for another one. He eyed the factory again. The first-floor windows were closed and protected by grates, but the upper windows were open and he could hear the faint hum of the machinery inside. Attached to one end of the factory, the end the crowd was on, was a guard shack. It was a small building, mostly windows, and above it, was a suspended covered walkway joining the factory to a three-story office building.

Day after day, he showed up at 5:30 in the morning at the corner of Champlain and Chestnut streets, joining a group of hungry people in the dark. Steam floated out of their mouths as they chatted, but he was in no mood to talk.

"There's a foreman!" someone shouted.

Every face turned toward the guard shack as people shouted things like, "Hire me! I'm a die setter!", "Hire me! I'm a production worker!"

Vern stood on his tip toes and waved his hiring card high above his head. "Hire me! I'm a punch press operator!" he yelled, hoping his voice was louder than the others.

A guard scanned the restless swarm, cupped his hands around his mouth and yelled, "We need a set-up man."

Groans could be heard as Vern lowered his arm, bumping a man that was pushing past him.

"Right here!" the man yelled. He was shoving his way through the tight horde, as if he were furiously digging for gold.

Another man rushed to the guard shack, holding out a carton of eggs and bowing to the foreman.

Someone from the crowd yelled, "Pot licker!"

"Who said that?" the guard asked.

The nasty name fit the man. Vern was sick of people like him, offering all sorts of foods and valuables to the foremen and the guards. It was a conniving way to work yourself into a job and he didn't have anything to offer.

"Who said that?" the guard repeated.

Vern had seen that guard before. He was one of three who worked the morning shift and each day those three men became meaner and more vicious. He watched as the guard pulled a billy from his belt loop, then disappear into the crowd.

Within moments, Vern caught sight of a billy, swinging through the air.

A sudden thud silenced the crowd.

5

CASPER

THE PUNCH PRESS machine was silent. A set-up man was busily working, hanging a card and adjusting the machine's meter. Casper glanced at the card, then looked at a chart on the wall. Production for the week was updated and recorded every morning and every name and number was in red, even Hank the Hoof's. He squinted at the card, but couldn't make out the piecework goal.

"Can you read it?" Joe asked.

"No," he replied. "Can you?"

"I think it says 1200, but I'm not sure."

In the middle of the floor was a desk. It was messy, caged in and dwarfed by the surrounding colossal machines. Behind the desk was the foreman.

"I hope he picks me," Joe said.

Casper was thinking the same thing as he slid forward and planted his feet. If it was a race to the machine, he knew he'd win. He waited and watched as the foreman approached the set-up man.

"I just *gotta* work this week," Joe added.

His voice sounded desperate, about as desperate as Casper felt. They were all capable punch press operators, every single one of them, but since Ford pulled out, jobs were few.

"Hey, pssst."

Casper looked at the end of the bench. It was Charlie. He was pointing at each man sitting there when he quietly said, "We're meeting at my house tonight." Then he mouthed the words *be there*.

6

EDITH

"What are you typing?" Genevieve asked.

Edith glanced at figures on a coffee stained paper. Her boss told her to type up the numbers exactly as they were written, but she knew he'd come back with some changes. "The numbers from yesterday," she replied.

"I doubt those workers made the Sixty B's. They're terrible workers."

It was Doris, the third secretary. She had an abrupt way about her that had startled Edith from the very first day.

"One man *almost* made it," Edith replied. "He was really close."

Out of the corner of her eye, she could see Doris's head shaking.

"Well," Doris snapped. "If they weren't doggin' around, they just might make the numbers."

Edith wondered how long it took Genevieve to get used to Doris and took a quick glance at her workmate. She was glancing back.

"And, my goodness" Doris added, "they need to be more careful. Especially the workers of Department Two."

Edith was supposed to get a tour of the factory when she

started, but that never happened. She knew a covered walkway connected her building to the factory and on a recent trip to the lady's room, she took a detour. The entrance to the walkway had a door that sometimes was open and on that day, it was. She quickly walked across the bridge and was about to reach for the factory door when it whooshed open. Startled, she fumbled for words when a gruff looking man marched into the space. But he passed by her without notice. The door was slowly closing and gave her a brief look inside. Glimpsing as much as she could, she gawked at the enormous machines operating at a brisk pace. They looked powerful and brutal as she watched them slam down like mechanized sledge hammers making loud noises. And, just as she spotted the men on the bench, the door closed.

"Those machines," Edith said, "look dangerous."

"It's just piecework," Doris replied. "You know, doing the same thing over and over again. How hard can that be?"

She thought of the scary machines and the speed at which the metal was cut.

"They're running awfully fast," she said. "It seems dangerous to keep raising the numbers. If they can't make the *first* Sixty B's, how are they gonna make the higher numbers?"

"Edith!" Doris's voice cracked. "Mr. Miniger is fair and honest."

She cringed, unsure of what line she crossed.

"Doris," Genevieve gently said, "she's not saying he isn't."

"Then why is she questioning things?"

"She's new and learning," Genevieve replied.

"Well—" Doris abruptly stopped.

The sound of footsteps echoed in the hall and quieted the room. Edith listened to the gait as it got louder. On her first day, she memorized her boss's footsteps. He had a hitch in his walk, making one foot sound louder than the other.

"Edith?"

Her boss's voice was distinct, too. Hoarse, yet strong. When she met him, she thought he had a cold, but soon realized he was a smoker. She looked at the doorway. His uneven hips made his stance crooked, but his posture was straight and severe.

"Yes, Mr. Moore?" she replied.

"Is the report done?"

Glancing at her work, she pulled the completed report from her typewriter.

He grabbed the paper, eyed the numbers and said, "I'll get back to you if anything needs to be amended."

She knew what that meant. There *would* be changes. Her grandmother said he was named right. 'Mr. Moore, and more, and more'.

He hobbled from the room, his footsteps sounding fainter and fainter.

"I'm taking these envelopes downstairs," Genevieve said. "Can I take anything for either of you?"

Edith shook her head and thought about her next task when suddenly, out of nowhere, a scream shot into the room, coming from the covered walkway. Its high pitched, animal like sound siphoned away her breath.

"See," Doris said. "They need to be more careful."

7

CASPER

THE PUNCH PRESS machine was splattered with blood. Sitting on the plate was the end of a finger.

Casper jumped from the bench and raced over to Joe.

The man was holding his wrist as his hand violently shook, and, while he screamed, the foreman was ranting about the stopped punch press.

Casper wrapped his arm around Joe's back and with Charlie's help they led him to the bench.

"Sit," Charlie said.

Joe fell back into the bench. "Another finger gone," he cried.

Casper pulled out his handkerchief and looked at the bloody stump. He winced at the sight of two wiggling tendons and blood pulsing from an opening where a finger used to be.

"Here," he said. "Use this."

The men of Department Two offered their handkerchiefs as Charlie began to bundle the stump.

"It's broken!" the foreman shouted.

"It's not broken," Hank said. "It's missing."

"I'm not talking about the finger," the foreman replied. "The punch press. *It's* broken."

Casper looked at the foreman. He was surveying the machine, hands on hips, shaking his head in disgust. Then he marched over to Joe and said, "Ring out. You're fired."

8

EDITH

"I NEED to order five hundred canisters of tear gas."

Edith froze. She must've heard incorrectly. She knew she shouldn't be eavesdropping, but Doris was on the telephone and they were the only two people in the office.

"Yes," Doris continued, "by Mr. Minch."

Slyly moving a pencil from one side of her desk to the other, Edith quickly peeked at Doris. A bun held the woman's graying red hair and two tight curls were pinned on top. The severe hairstyle matched the deep creases around her mouth and, although she wore red lipstick, she looked quite hardened.

"That's right," Doris said, "five hundred canisters."

Edith tried to look away, but couldn't. She watched as Doris sifted through papers, her gaze bouncing from sheet to sheet, when suddenly, the woman was staring straight at Edith.

Her heart pounded as she turned toward her typewriter and banged her fingers on any of the keys.

"We appreciate it," Doris said and hung up. "And you."

Letters and symbols appeared on a paper as Edith kept moving her fingers from key to key and row to row.

"I'm talking to you," Doris said.

She heard herself swallow, but didn't look up.

"Look. At. Me," Doris demanded.

Little by little, Edith turned her head.

The woman was standing with one hand on her hip, the other holding a pencil and pointing at her. "This is confidential," she said. "You know what that means, right?"

She felt herself slowly nod, unable to look away from Doris's endless stare. The woman's glare was piercing and unblinking as she picked up papers, tapped them on the desk, then walked out.

The room was empty.

Dust particles floated, drifting downward when Genevieve came in.

"You okay?" she asked. "Looks like you've seen a ghost."

Edith just sat there.

"What did Doris say now?" Genevieve asked.

"She—" Edith stopped. Doris did say it was confidential. Maybe that included Genevieve.

"Come on," Genevieve said. "What did she say?"

"I'm not sure if I should tell you," Edith replied. Then in a lower voice she added, "Doris said it was confidential."

"Confidential for *other* people," Genevieve replied. "I'm a secretary. I *have to* know these things."

"Well, I'm not sure I heard her right," Edith said.

"You heard her right. Now, come on. What did she say?"

"She was ordering *five hundred tear gas canisters*," Edith whispered. "For Mr. Minch."

It was almost certain the misunderstanding would make Genevieve laugh, but her workmate was quiet.

"I know he's a tough boss," Edith said, "but—"

"There's talk of another strike," Genevieve whispered.

Before Edith started working at Auto-Lite, she heard about a strike in February. Some of the men from Department Two walked out, held picket signs and marched in front of the factory. It only lasted five days and, whatever the issues were, it seemed things got resolved.

"I thought the February strike solved everything," she said. "Everyone was so happy when it ended. And, it was a quick strike, right?"

"Yes. It lasted only five days," Genevieve whispered. "Mr. Minch said he'd recognized the union. But he didn't. He only said that to get the men back to—"

Her sentence abruptly stopped at the sound of footsteps in the hallway.

9

CASPER

CASPER FOLLOWED the men of his department out the factory side door. The moment he stepped outside, cold April air smacked him in the face. He took a deep breath letting the chill bite his throat and lungs. Slowly, he exhaled, watching his steamy breath disappear.

Trudging from the building to the factory gate, he trailed behind his fellow punch press operators. They were all young men, like him, bundled in tweed caps and wool coats, but they looked like old field hands, beaten from a harvesting day.

Joe's exposed tissue and bone flashed in his mind.

They passed the guard shack, one after another. Glancing at one of the guards, he received a cordial nod. He nodded back knowing the man would easily replace him with a fresh, young body from the waiting crowd. Most of the older men had already been fired for sickness or injuries or giving an opinion, and, although he was only twenty-five, he was nearing the top age of the new hires. The group of waiting people wanted what he had and every day more people showed up. He easily felt desperate spirits by the uncomfortable way the people didn't look at him. He didn't want to look at them either, but spotted a few men with dyed hair.

The punch press operators had to make their way through the crowd. People were reluctant to lose their spots. Casper wanted to push them, push them hard and all the way to Lagrange Street. But, eventually, a path formed and they made their way to the edge of the sidewalk.

Slow moving automobiles crept along Champlain Street. He stopped and waited, listening to the factory noises as the shift changed. Car after car passed by, leaving swirls of exhaust. Finally, there was an opening between two Model T's. When he stepped onto the brick road, his foot twisted in a crevice. A fitting end for the day.

By the time he reached the other side of the street, most of the men had disappeared into the parking lot. Within minutes, the area was in transition. He eyed the billboards lining the back of the lot and scoffed at the image of new car and overcoat. One of the billboards was advertising soap using a larger-than-life handprint. Joe's mutilated finger flashed in his mind again.

He was headed home, walking south on Chestnut Street. The quaint neighborhood usually offered a peaceful retreat, but not today. There was no satisfaction in familiar streets, or trees rustling, or friendly hellos. No satisfaction in knowing every alleyway, lamppost, or parking sign. Even the thought of Buckeye Brewery didn't make him happy.

An oncoming car forced him onto the sidewalk. He kicked a stone out of his way, ricocheting it off a tree trunk and back at his shin. He tried to think about how living so close saved precious gas money, money he wasn't earning. Then the exposed punch press slamming down on Joe's finger flashed in his mind again.

"Casp!"

He heard a familiar voice calling him.

"Wait up!" it said.

He stopped and turned around to see Charlie heading toward him. The man was trudging up the slight incline known as 'Chestnut Hill'.

"Don't forget," Charlie said, "eight o'clock, my house."

He thought about the covert meeting and his wife's opposition to a union. And, how she said they were made up of thugs and triggermen. He wasn't sure what they were about either, but after today, he was going to find out.

10

EDITH

EDITH'S SPEEDY TYPING SLOWED, then stopped. Her boss had approached her desk asking if the modified report was done. He was tapping a pen into his open palm as if that would speed her up. She looked at his notes one more time when she heard a male voice from the hallway ask, "Is it done?"

The tapping of her boss's pen ceased. "Hurry up," he whispered.

She banged out more numbers.

"Well?" the voice said.

Just as her boss reached for the paper, she typed the last number. The report was pulled free, spinning the typewriter platen with a zip. A quick glance at the doorway and she spotted the man. He was a thin middle-aged man with graying black hair. His suit was nice, very nice. Double breasted, with sharp pleats. From the way Genevieve and Doris were pretending they were busy, she knew he was important.

"Um."

That was all her boss said, a stumbling syllable. She looked up at him. He was staring down at the paper as if there was a mistake. But she knew there was no mistake.

"Bring it here," the man said.

Edith started to stand up, but her boss had turned away and was heading toward the doorway. "Yes, Mr. Minch," he said.

Her breath shortened at the thought of finally seeing *the notorious Mr. Minch.* After all, he was the Vice President of the company and had a reputation for being quite harsh. Or, as Genevieve liked to say, 'he knew how to tighten the screws better than anyone'.

The paper was shaking in her boss's hand as the man grabbed at it. She glanced at Genevieve, but she was busily writing on a notepad.

"These numbers," Mr. Minch said, "they need to be raised."

Edith stared at the back of her boss. His severe stance was now a slumped posture and he wasn't speaking or telling the vice president that raising the numbers was all wrong.

"Your foremen," Mr. Minch continued, "they need to get more ornery."

Her boss remained silent, his head lowered.

"If they can't do it," Mr. Minch added, "we'll find somebody who can."

Edith looked at Genevieve who was furiously writing something. Then she looked at Doris. The woman was rifling through a desk drawer as if there was money in it. Then she looked at her boss. He still wasn't moving or telling the man that the workers could *never* make those numbers.

"And," Mr. Minch said, "one of the presses stopped this week. *Twice.*"

The way he said twice was way too calm, causing a feathery shiver to touch her neck. She wanted to shake her boss, make him speak, but he was looking at the floor.

"Raise those numbers," Mr. Minch demanded.

Her boss was nodding.

"Say something!" she silently screamed. Tell him about the worker whose finger got chopped off or about how a man was fired for throwing up. She opened her mouth to speak, but saw Genevieve swiftly look in her direction and discretely shake her head.

"Listen to me," Mr. Minch said. He was tapping his finger against her boss's chest. "Those men better not be talking about a union anymore. Got it?"

11

CASPER

SMALL RECTANGULAR WINDOWS in Charlie's basement added little light to the candlelit space. As Charlie spoke, Casper spotted the crescent moon through a window above the man's head. He had been talking to the men of Department Two for a while, discussing the advantages of joining a union. The men were sitting on the edges of their chairs and nodding. Charlie had a way about him, everybody knew it. He could present any situation as a *light at the end of the tunnel*. And this evening was no different.

Casper sunk his elbows into his knees and leaned forward. Eyeing his cigarette, he put it to his lips and took a satisfying drag. He used to smoke Luckies, a deck a day, until Clement Miniger, the Auto-Lite President, appeared in one of the ads and all the men of Department Two immediately started rolling their own. Tilting his head back, he pursed his lips and exhaled. A thin trail of smoke weaved its way to exposed ceiling pipes.

"Men," Charlie said, "this will only work if we trust in one another."

"But if the strike in February didn't work, how will *this* one?"

Bill, a punch press operator, had joined the conversation. The man was looking gallant tonight, wearing a suit and tie, just like one of the Auto-Lite managers. When he first arrived, there was a shared gasp from the group until he explained his appearance and his wife's belief he was going to church. But, his question was valid and Casper was wondering the same thing.

"Men, we're gaining momentum," Charlie said. "It won't be just us, the unholy thirteen. This time, we have *all* of Department Two and a lot of the production workers. Not only the men, but the women. And again, Spicer, Logan, Bingham and City Auto."

Casper watched as Charlie named the surrounding Toledo manufacturing companies, using his three fingers and a stub. He thought about the strike in February, when a handful of workers from those companies coordinated with the men from Department Two and collectively walked out. Production slowed and management quickly agreed to recognize a union, except for Miniger and Minch, the Auto-Lite executives. If it wasn't for the persuasiveness of Local 18384's business agent, Thomas Ramsey, the men of Department Two would have lost the strike *and* their jobs. Ramsey convinced the striking workers from the other companies it *had to be* all or none before anyone returned to work and Auto-Lite's management *must* recognize the union.

Casper remembered the five days in February, in single digit weather. Union badges and picket signs made them look official, but they had to huddle around drum fires in front of the factory to keep warm. Pressure must've been applied to Miniger and Minch because they finally agreed to recognize the union and the men returned to work.

"But last strike," Bill said, "Minch agreed to recognize the union. But thirty days later, he didn't."

"We're not asking for a lot," Charlie replied. "just livable wages, a safer factory and recognition for our time working there. It's basic rights."

Charlie paced the floor before continuing.

"This ain't gonna be easy," he said. "But, Ramsey said section 7(a) of the NIRA states we *can* form Local 18384. And, if anyone can help us, he can."

Casper thought of the National Industrial Recovery Act. It was established in 1933, last year, and favored the workers.

"But Minch is a son of a bitch," Hank said, "He'll just hire our replacements."

Hank the Hoof, Casper's best friend, always telling it like it is.

"We make stampings for the entire assembly," Charlie replied. "And, now, we have the *entire* department ready to strike. Without us, they *cannot* run the plant."

The room shifted with Charlie's words, not with uneasiness, but enthusiasm.

Casper leaned back in an old chair and thought about the situation. Ramsey was quite the man, and if he could do everything he said, the bench would no longer be the only safe place in the factory.

"We can't go on like this," Charlie continued. "Piecework doesn't pay. If you make the high quota, you don't get the full amount, not even close. And I don't have to remind you of the unsafe conditions."

"But," Joe interjected. "What do we really *know* about unions?"

Joe had been quietly sitting at the meeting. His hand was bandaged and he looked woozy, but he was there.

"They're able to protect workers," Charlie said. "Like you. They won't allow a fella to be fired for getting injured. Or if a machine breaks. The union will back us. And, no more 'Little Red Apple Boys' bribing their way into our jobs."

Words like *pot licker* and *suck up* filled the air.

"With a union," Charlie continued, "the company will recognize us and our time there. We'll have seniority. And safety plates will be added to the machines. Plus, no more using our own tools."

Casper inhaled the last of his cigarette, thinking of his broken micrometer.

"What about using the toilet?" Bill asked.

Normally, a question like that would make the group laugh, except the raw memory of one of the men being dragged from the toilet by a foreman, pants down, didn't seem very funny.

"Yeah, we're gonna be able to use the john when we need it," Charlie replied. "Men, the *Auto-Lite Council* was management's response to the first strike. *Their* union. If that's what you want to call it. This time, they're gonna recognize *our* union."

Casper stubbed his cigarette into an ashtray as he thought about the Auto-Lite Council. It was run by company men and they were not concerned with factory conditions or wages, at all.

"Men," Charlie added, "we don't wanna be recognized by our missing fingers, but by our skill. *Our* department has power. But, we *must* stick together, that's the only way this is gonna work."

Pledge cards and applications were handed out. Casper's was already filled out, despite his wife's hesitation.

"And, don't forget what Ramsey said," Charlie added, "that the picket line is our ultimate weapon to make a change."

12

VERN

VERN PLANTED his feet firmly in front of the crowd. He had to push his way through, elbow a few people and throw his weight around, but now, he was standing in front. And, no one was going to move him. He was closer to the guard shack than he'd ever been before. Close enough to clearly see their faces through the windows. He had been holding up his hiring card, trying to get their attention all morning, but they never looked his way.

"I want a job!" came a shout from someone in the crowd.

There had been shouts all morning, as usual. A few scuffles, too. But Vern reserved his most aggressive self for when a foreman appeared at the factory front doors. That meant a job just opened and that everyone was on the offense.

The morning shift was already inside and the parking lot across the street was full. He desperately needed gas money and was tired of walking. Today was his day and he was going to get a job.

He glanced at the guards again. The smugness of the way they drank their coffee and smoked their endless supply of cigarettes made him want to spit. If it wasn't for their powerful influence on who got a job, he might have walked right up there, smashed a window and grabbed the coffee right out of their hands. He started to fantasize about doing just that when a Cadillac V16 Landaulette De Luxe pulled up to the gate and stopped right in front of him.

The guards were hustling out of the shack as Vern eyed the fancy maroon vehicle. In the center of each white-walled tire was a shiny, silver cap reflecting a warped, vagabond crowd. There was a driver, wearing a chauffeur hat, and a hidden passenger in the back.

Suddenly, Vern felt the crowd surge forward.

"Mr. Miniger! Mr. Miniger," they shouted. "Hire me! Hire me!"

He was pushed into the driveway and closer to the vehicle. Holding his hands out, he braced for impact, but stopped himself from touching the car.

The gate was opening and the Cadillac was inching forward, giving Vern a view of the backseat. He had heard about Mr. Miniger, the President of the Auto-Lite factory *and*, the vice president named Mr. Minch. Their names sounded so much alike, that he constantly got them mixed up. He'd never met either man before, but the nasty things people said about the two apparently applied to both. He peered inside the car and spotted a man in the back. He was reading a newspaper, in a sophisticated way, wearing a black overcoat that contrasted with stark white hair.

Adrenaline surged through Vern as he took his hiring pass and pressed it against the window. Leaning in, he said, "Mr. Miniger, I'm a punch press operator. I'm ready to work."

He waited for the man to look up and get a good view of his qualification, but he kept on reading.

"Get away from there," a guard shouted.

Vern tapped the glass and yelled to the man, when suddenly, the engine roared. Within moments, the car was in the factory yard, having kicked up a pebble that stung Vern in the shin.

The gate closed when he heard someone say, “My hiring card expires tomorrow.”

“Good,” he mumbled.

Returning to his stance, he let out a sigh and elbowed somebody for good measure. Then he fixed his gaze on the factory entrance. Glass double doors reflected headlamps and radiators from the parking lot across the street. He watched the doors and waited and waited, until finally one of the doors opened. A gruff looking foreman appeared and motioned to the guards.

People shouted, announcing their need for a job and what position they held. Vern tried to yell the loudest. “I’m a punch press operator!” he shouted.

A guard cupped his hands over his mouth and said, “We need a production worker. A strong man!”

Vern shoved his hiring card in his pocket, puffed out his chest and shouted, “I’m strong!”

To his surprise, the guard walked over to him.

Vern nodded to the man and said, “I’ll take it!”

“You,” the guard said.

He quickly stepped forward. “Thank you! Thank you,” he said.

“Not you,” the guard replied. “Him.”

Vern turned around. A husky young man, maybe fifteen years old, was the recipient of the guard’s random selection.

“Are you strong?” the guard asked.

The young man raced up to the foreman, then dropped down on the sidewalk and began doing pushups.

“You’ll do,” the foreman said.

13

CASPER

"I'M gonna ask Minch for a meeting," Charlie quietly said.

Casper heard that before. Charlie was always trying to meet with the VP, thinking he could reason with him. A few times, *very few times*, he was granted permission. The meetings never resulted in anything. But Charlie kept trying.

"He's just gonna tell you the same thing," Casper replied. "He's not gonna change his mind. Or this place."

"I know," Charlie said. "Call me an optimist, but I'm gonna try again."

How anyone could be an optimist in this day and age and working for Auto-Lite was beyond Casper. All he could focus on was putting one foot in front of the other. Things were bad. His mortgage was in arrears; his cupboards were bare and his father-in-law was sick. Every time he thought things were getting better, they got worse.

He glanced at the clock. It was almost noon and he hadn't rung in yet. Neither had Bill, or Hank or Charlie. At that moment, he was watching Lester sweat and hustle, working the punch press like a bean shooter. The man was about to make Sixty B's when he ran out of pieces and the foreman made him ring out.

“See that?” Charlie asked. “That’s the type of thing we’re gonna fix. It’s not Lester’s fault there ain’t enough pieces to run through.”

He looked Charlie. He was a small man, boy like, and known as ‘Little Charlie’. When he sat on the bench, his feet barely touched the wooden floor. But, his spirited personality made him larger than most people.

“I’m gonna try again,” Charlie said, “explain our position. If he loses our department, he’ll lose production. And, if he doesn’t listen, we’re ready to—”

Casper didn’t hear his last word and looked at his friend. He was smiling and looking back at him when he silently mouthed the last word.

14

VERN

VERN WALKED past the factory and it's early morning crowd. He was hungry and his wife's supper didn't have enough calories to sustain even his youngest son. Yesterday, he overheard someone talking about cheap donuts and free coffee at the corner beer joint. He had already walked nineteen blocks from his house to the factory and the cold, dark, April morning wasn't going to stop him from walking a few blocks further. He touched the single coin in his pocket, hoping that would buy him something. He had been to Buckeye Brewery before, when they were bottling ginger ale and root beer, but since prohibition had been lifted, he didn't have any money to buy a beer.

On the other side of the street, next to the factory building, was a group of women. They were standing in front of the double glass doors, probably waiting for a foreman. He knew he should be waiting too, but his stomach kept growling.

He passed the parking lot, already full of cars, and eyed the billboards at the back of the lot. A new car, an overcoat, soap, and coffee. Fresh, rich coffee. His mouth watered.

Passing the hiring building, he quickened his gait and contemplated the additional three blocks.

Vehicle headlights were coming down the road and soon, a Buckeye Brewing truck was by his side. Stacks of beer cases shook and rattled on the open bed as the truck rumbled over the brick road. It would be easy to grab one of the cases and run, dull his mind for a day or two, but he stayed on the sidewalk.

Glancing at the corner street signs, he crossed over Magnolia Street. A long building, belonging to the brewery company, was on the next block. His legs felt heavy as he walked past the hodgepodge red brick of continuous linking structures thinking of a doughy treat.

As daybreak neared, he stopped at the corner of Champlain and Bush streets. A cartoon 'Bucky' billboard, towel in one arm and tray of beer in the other, was on top of a brick building. Eyeing two more Brewery trucks, he stepped over the railroad tracks and dashed across the street.

His pace accelerated and, soon, he was at the corner bar. Grabbing the entrance handle, he practically flung himself inside.

The room was full for the early hour, almost appearing as evening, and the men and women were talking about something serious. Scanning the room, his eyes landed on a side table with a plate of only one donut. He approached the dish.

An older man appeared on the other side of the bar, ladling steaming fritters from a pot. "Mornin'," he said.

Vern nodded, but didn't take his eyes off the growing pyramid of baked goods.

"Careful," the man said, "they're hot."

He stood there, staring at the food.

"Here," the man said, handing him a plate. "No charge t'day. Take as many as you want."

Vern grabbed three and bit into the first one. The hot

steamy dough singed the roof of his mouth as the man handed him a glass of water.

"Told ya they're hot," he said.

Vern tried to say 'thanks' but the sticky treat made it sound like a belch.

"You're new here, aren't ya," the man asked.

He nodded and gulped the water.

"Eat up," the man said. "We got more a comin'."

The next donut was as good as the first, sweet and thick, and he couldn't chew it fast enough. Swallowing hard, he swigged more water. The third donut was almost gone, when he overheard a conversation.

"They're gonna strike again."

"And give up their jobs?"

He looked at the bar. A group of men wearing tattered work clothes were deep into the discussion.

"That's risky 'cuz all the people outta work."

"I heard that factory chops off fingers. And, they sit for hours just waiting for work."

"A bad job is better than no job. I'm goin' over and see what's goin' on."

Quickly, Vern grabbed another donut and dashed out the door.

15

EDITH

"I'M GOING TO THE LADIES' room," Genevieve said.

Edith was left alone in the secretaries' office. It was a peaceful afternoon since Doris was called to the mailroom.

She stopped typing and looked at the closed curtains. Tranquil light filtered through, reflecting softly on the file cabinets and desk tops making her wonder if spring was close. Stepping to the window, she parted the curtains and looked outside. Bright green buds covered the tree tops and puffy clouds floated in the sky. It was as peaceful outside as it was inside. Even the people waiting for a job seemed calmer than usual. The parking lot across the street was motionless, the billboards colorful and pleasant. She glanced at the automobile advertisement, thinking of how Genevieve said she looked like the lady in the ad. Today, she fixed her hair to match the picture outside.

Footsteps clicked in the hallway. They were loud and purposeful and not Genevieve's or Doris's. Quickly, she returned to her desk.

"Pardon me, Ma'am."

It was a man wearing a dark blue uniform and knee high boots, standing in the doorway with his hat in his hand.

"I'm Sheriff Krieger," he said. "And you are?"

Before she could reply or extend an invitation, he walked into the room. The repetitive heaviness of each footsteps sounded like a sledgehammer pounding the wooden floor.

"I'm Edith Johnson," she replied.

He was walking toward Genevieve's desk. It was unsettling the way he didn't stop moving, and now he seemed to be circling in on something. She glanced at different parts of his uniform: a polished badge, shiny gun grip and dangling billy club. She was at a loss about what to do. He was by Genevieve's typewriter, looking at her notepad, when he stopped.

"Can I help you with something?" she asked.

He didn't answer. Instead, he touched the notepad and looked at the front page. A bald spot on the top of his head reflected the glare from the windows. Then, abruptly, the glare was gone as he headed toward Doris's desk.

"Are you a secretary?" he asked.

He was circling that desk too, the same way he did Genevieve's. She didn't know if she should stop him or not.

"Yes," she replied.

He was now picking up Doris's notepad and reading it.

Worry fluttered in her stomach as she listened for her workmate's footsteps, but the hallway was silent.

"And, what are *you* working on?" he asked.

Why did he need to know what she was working on? She didn't think that was any of his business, but answered him anyway. "A list of names for my boss," she said.

He opened one of Doris's desk drawers and asked, "Who's your boss?"

Alarm bells rang in her head as if a fire were in the room. She stuttered an answer. "Mr. ah, Mr. Moore," she replied.

Suddenly, he was on the move again. His gait was heavier and quicker than before and heading toward her desk. She wanted to pull the cover over her typewriter, but it was too late. He was standing right there.

"Who's the lady?" he said, nodding to the picture on her desk.

She fidgeted with a pencil and glanced at the doorway. "My grandmother," she replied.

"Pretty," he said. "You look like her."

He was now at the window, her window, looking outside at her view.

The room was silent.

She strained to hear if anyone was in the hallway when an abrupt, booming voice said, "There you are, you ol' son of a bitch."

It was Mr. Minch.

"I told you I'd be here," the Sheriff replied.

Edith watched the two men shake hands like old classmates.

"We've got a lot to discuss," Mr. Minch said.

16

CASPER

ANOTHER CANDLELIT MEETING WAS UNDERWAY. Casper sat on the steps to Charlie's basement, about midway up. There were a lot of people crammed into the space, sitting in every chair and lined against the walls.

"You gals on the circuit breaker line," Charlie said. "We're glad you're joining us. Next meeting is at Memorial Hall, with Spicer, Bingham, Logan and City Auto workers. Tom Ramsey is makin' Local 18384 official."

"What's next?" someone asked.

"I'm gonna try to talk to Minch," Charlie said. "Give it one more try."

That name was all he had to say. The room was motivated and everyone was booing. Casper cupped his hands around his mouth, angled his head upward and booed the loudest.

"I know, I know," Charlie said. "But *if* we can solve this without a strike, then we can keep working."

"Miniger and Minch," one of the women said, "they're not gonna allow *our* union. They want us to join *their* union, the Auto-Lite Council."

Casper scoffed at the idea of a company's own ambassador representing the very workers they wanted to silence and said, "They must think we're idiots."

"Yeah," Lester added. "One of *their* suck-ups looking out for us? Never."

"We have the numbers," Charlie said. "And, I'm gonna let Minch know it. He'll have one. More. Shot. And, if he doesn't agree to our demand—"

The room went silent.

"Get ready," Charlie added. "We're goin' on strike."

17

EDITH

THE WALK to the lady's room took Edith past Mr. Minch's office. Thankfully, like always, his door was closed. Mr. Miniger, the president of Auto-Lite, had an office on the second floor. She hadn't met him yet, but Genevieve said he was an old sweetheart and always gave the office employees a big Christmas bonus.

"He's a Communist!"

Abrupt words coming from Mr. Minch's office no longer startled her. Even with his door closed, she knew it was him. His outbursts about Communists or Bolsheviks were common. She wondered if anything ever made him happy.

"I'm not meeting with him," she heard him shout. "They can strike for all I care. There's plenty of labor out there and we have a stockpile of ammunition."

Ammunition?

The unexpected word made her shudder. Tear gas and, now, ammunition. She had no idea what was happening and ran back to her desk.

"Running a race?" Genevieve asked.

Edith looked around the room. It was only she and Genevieve.

"Mr. Minch is shouting," she whispered

"Now what?" Genevieve asked.

"He said they have a stockpile of . . . *ammunition.*"

Genevieve didn't say anything.

Edith stared at her, wondering why she wasn't speaking.

"What is going on?" she asked.

It was obvious they were the only two in the office, but Genevieve still looked around the room. Edith watched her pause and, only after a few long moments, she finally spoke.

"Things are getting bad," Genevieve whispered.

"What do you mean '*things*'?" Edith asked.

"Just things."

"Like what?"

The awkward silence was back. Edith watched as Genevieve leaned back in her chair, and exhaled a long, slow breath.

"Tell me," Edith said.

Genevieve glanced at the doorway, then in a very quiet voice said, "One of the workers wanted to meet with Mr. Minch. But, as you've heard, he's not interested."

"What did he want to meet about?"

"I don't know, but I think they're gonna strike again."

"But I thought you said Mr. Miniger was going to make everything better."

"All I know," Genevieve added, "is that *if they do strike*, Mr. Minch is planning on hiring replacements."

Edith thought of the waiting crowd outside and how it was growing larger every day and how they were desperate to work for anyone, including Mr. Minch.

"Then why is he talking about ammunition?" she asked.

"I don't know," Genevieve replied. "I just don't know."

PART II

The man who has his millions will want everything he can lay his hands on and then raise his voice against the poor devil who wants ten cents more a day.
~ Samuel Gompers

18

VERN

VERN COULDN'T BELIEVE he was getting ready for work. Last night, the man on the telephone asked him if he had a measuring gauge. It was needed for the job. Vern said he had one, but he didn't. A year ago it was sold for food.

He was told to drive to the factory, park across the street, and a guard would escort him into the building. He was nervous. The first few weeks of the strike, he stood with the pickets, hiding the true reason he was there. They were angry and talked about the unsafe conditions and pathetic wages. But what surprised him most was their willingness to bet their only income source on the *hopes* that Auto-Lite would concede. Whenever he spoke to one of them, he tried to sound agreeable, but their suspicious looks made him stop going.

Fueled by borrowed gas money, his Model T rattled and shook as he drove through Toledo. He was on Lagrange Street, heading south and Champlain Street was the next left. Thinking about the strikers, he took a deep breath and turned the corner.

The organized picket line was gone.

To his alarm, a dense mob was in its place, starting at

Elm Street, two full blocks from the factory. People were packed on sidewalks, front yards, and part of the road. Slowly, he drove down the street. His heart was thumping as he approached the crowd and, within seconds, the pickets had surrounded his car. Their faces were inches from his window and their fists banged on his glass.

"Scab!" they shouted. "Go home!"

When he didn't stop, a man pounded on his hood so hard, he felt it through the steering wheel.

Carefully, he pressed on, moving inch by inch, when suddenly, a path appeared. Armed guards had parted the crowd, giving a car in front of him a way to the factory. He followed closely and finally, he was in the parking lot.

Gripping the borrowed measuring gauge, he started to open his door when a couple of pickets pushed it closed and trapped him inside.

He looked at the crowd. People were everywhere and no escort was in sight.

Without warning, his car started to rock. Then, suddenly, it stopped and the pickets left his side. A fight had broken out, creating a momentary diversion.

Quickly, he slipped outside.

"You should be ashamed of yourself!" a woman shouted.

Warm, gooey spit hit him in the jaw as he lowered his head and began to barrel into the crowd. Hands landed on his back and shoulders, pushing him in one direction, then another. He almost fell when a space abruptly opened.

"Make way!" a man said.

He didn't look up, but knew a guard was clearing a path for him.

19

CASPER

HANK the Hoof was shouting at a picket, a picket who was talking to one of the guards. Usually, everyone kept their distance from those guards, but that guy walked right up to the guard shack.

Casper eyed the picket. It was someone he did not recognize. Surprisingly, many sympathizers had joined their strike and, most days, he lost track of his fellow punch press operators. In April, when the strike first started, the picket line was an actual line with strikers wearing badges, holding signs and marching in an orderly fashion. Charlie had pleaded with the existing group waiting to be hired, explaining the treacherous conditions inside and measly paycheck, insufficient for any human being. He emphasized how the invisible picket line shouldn't be crossed. But those people didn't listen and kept showing up, so they were heckled and called *scabs* and *slugs*, and, soon enough, the scabs did not return.

It was already the middle of May. Days turned into weeks, quicker than Casper liked. He thought the strike was going to put a dent in production and be over quickly. But new employees arrived every day, parked across from the factory and were escorted into the building. Miniger and Minch gave the guards ammunition and guns. And, rumors circulated that the sheriff had deputized untrained men and gave them freedom to do anything.

Thomas Ramsey, the union's business agent, tried to keep things on task. Every day, he stood on the back of a pickup truck and shouted about fairness, safety and livable wages. The crowd's energy was already high and Ramsey's words brought additional motivation. But, Casper's fuel, the *real fuel*, was knowing the Electric Auto-Lite Co. was *not* suffering because they maintained a steady flow of new workers.

"This hiring has gotta stop," Charlie said. "I'm gonna meet with Minch again."

Casper lost hope, a long time ago, for Charlie's future meeting. Miniger and Minch were clearly thumbing their noses at the strikers. It was easy for them to find replacements. At first, Casper thought the new labor was coming from the Lucas County Unemployment League. But he was wrong. That group understood the horrible conditions more than anyone. They aligned with the strikers and stood with them in sympathy.

May's nice weather enticed an even larger crowd, numbering in the thousands. When the shifts changed, hostile banter easily flowed, the worst coming from the women pickets, but it did not stop the new recruits from showing up.

And now, Hank was yelling at one of the pickets. "You!" he shouted, "I asked you *what are ya doin'*?"

The guy turned around and was facing the crowd.

"Yeah. You!" Hank yelled.

Casper watched as Hank pushed through the crowd and stalked right up to the picket. He wondered what provoked Hank until he spotted a piece of paper in the man's hand. A quick move from Hank, and *he* was now holding the paper.

The guard didn't try to stop the scuffle, but grinned at the scene.

"What does it say?" someone shouted.

The picket tried to grab the note, swinging his hands as if he were reaching for money. But, Hank held out his long arm, keeping the man at a distance.

"It says," Hank began, "Please hire me. I'm a—"

Hank stopped. Casper eyed his buddy. His brow furrowed and his nostrils flared as read the final words and said, "Punch. Press. Operator."

The words swirled in Casper's mind as he thought of the violent machines chopping and pulling at fingers and thumbs as men were pushed to their limits trying to make fantastical goals for miserable wages. His body reacted automatically and pushed its way through the crowd. He shoved other angry pickets all moving forward, and by the time he reached the guy, he was already on the ground being punched and kicked.

Casper pushed his way in and knelt next to the man.

"Did you think you were gonna slip into our jobs unnoticed?" he shouted. Then slugged the guy in his side.

20

EDITH

"I THINK one of the pickets is in Mr. Minch's office," Edith said. She wouldn't have mentioned the matter, except Doris wasn't in the room.

"Really?" Genevieve replied.

"I think so. I heard someone call him Charlie."

For weeks, the strike had been going on. Her neighbor gave her a ride into work and each day they arrived, the crowd was larger and more aggressive.

She watched as Genevieve silently stood up and tiptoed to the doorway.

"What are you doing?" Edith asked.

"Come on," Genevieve whispered.

Quietly she got up and followed her workmate into the hall.

The space was empty and, as usual, the door to Mr. Minch's office was closed. Edith watched as Genevieve snuck up to his door and placed her ear against the wood. Then she motioned for Edith to join her.

Glancing down the hall, Edith eyed the closed doors, then tiptoed over to Genevieve and carefully leaned in.

"You've seen the size of the crowd," a male voice said,

"If you deputize some of *us*, we'll keep things under control an' work this out peacefully."

Knowing recently laid off Toledo policemen refused to join the sheriff's team, she pressed her ear closer to the door, waiting for an answer.

"I'm serious," the male voice said.

"Well, I'm serious, too."

That was Mr. Minch. His voice was very clear.

"Like I said the *last* time you were here," he continued. "We've got a million-dollar reserve set aside to break you strikers."

A million dollars.

Edith thought of the absurdity of stockpiling tear gas bombs and ammunition instead of using a fraction of that money to make the factory safe and pay the workers just a little bit more.

"Mr. Minch," the man said, "if you would just *recognize* the union, we could all get back to work and make *you* more money."

"As far as I'm concerned," Mr. Minch replied, "the strike is over. All the jobs are filled."

The room went quiet, very quiet. Edith held her breath listening for movement.

"Well then," the man said. "Get ready to spend that million dollars."

"You boys better watch yourselves," Mr. Minch added. "Can't fight the law."

"They ain't got enough paddy wagons to mass arrest us."

"Get the hell outta my office," Mr. Minch shouted.

Edith felt Genevieve's hand pushing at her shoulder as she whispered, "Go! Go!

21

CASPER

"NOBODY'S TALKIN' about Dillinger anymore. They're all talkin' about the strike."

Casper reached for a ketchup bottle as he listened to Virgil talk. The man owned the local lunch box, a small canteen near the factory, and always had words of encouragement. It didn't hurt that he gave out free hotdogs and coffee either.

"The whole city is behind you fellas," Virgil said.

It was true. It wasn't hard to notice hundreds of people showing up every day, always more than the day before, and sympathizing with them. He tipped the ketchup bottle over his plate and gave it a shake.

"Most of the policemen," Virgil continued, "they're on your side too. That's why Sheriff Krieger had to deputize men from outside the area. And, he deputized some of the Auto-Lite managers, too."

A quick shake of the bottle and the ketchup slowly poured. His mouth watered as he picked up the bun and bit into the dog.

"Why, just yesterday," Virgil said, "I saw a lady scab get kicked by a picket. And the policeman over there, well, he surely saw it too, but he turned the other way. Even *after* the lady complained."

Casper swallowed the much-appreciated food and said, "Did you see that newspaper article about Sheriff Krieger?"

"The apology letter?" Virgil asked. "Directly written to Minch where Krieger denied calling him *pretty tricky*?"

"Yeah, that one," Casper replied. "That suck-up changed his words and said Minch was a *capable company man*."

"Ah. Don't worry about that palooka," Virgil said. "Miniger helped him win his seat. He was *never* gonna be on your side."

Casper thought about Minch's cozy relationship with the sheriff and how the pickets were never going to be in a fair fight.

"You fellas keep doing what you're doing," Virgil added. "You *are* making changes."

22

VERN

VERN WAS STARING at a foreman's beefy, scarred hand as it pointed at his face.

"Ring in," the foreman said.

Despite his size, Vern sprung up from the bench, intending to run to the punch press machine, when a man stepped in front of him and cut him off. The move was so abrupt and intentional, Vern wanted to punch his face until he spotted a tiny box in the man's hand. It was being transferred to the foreman's.

"Hey," Vern snapped. "What's going on?"

A sweaty grimace on the foreman's face turned into a broad smile when he said, "Go ahead."

The man ran to the punch press and began to set up.

"Hey, suck-hole," Vern said. "It's my turn."

He was approaching the machine, when the foreman said, "Go sit down."

"But, it's my—"

Vern's sentence unexpectedly stopped as he felt a sharp tug at his arm and a voice in his ear. "Sit down," it said.

He looked at the hand and followed the arm to a face. It

was a set-up man, staring into his eyes when he repeated, "Just sit down. You'll get your chance."

Vern shrugged the hand away, wanting to claim *his* job when he felt the grip again.

"Don't do it," the set-up man quietly said. "If you do, they'll fire you."

He stopped. He was only a foot or two from the punch press, ready to make as many parts as he could. But, he knew his chance had slipped away.

The spot on the bench, his old spot, was still warm. He looked around the factory room. It was completely different from what he imagined. The factories he worked in before were organized. They weren't safe, but they were organized. This one, was disorganized *and* unsafe.

He leaned back, let out a long exhale, and listened to the rhythmic sound of the machines. They were clanging and rumbling and humming, when suddenly, a metal screech pierced the air. He scanned the floor eyeing a stopped punch press. *His* punch press. The suck-hole man was slapping the machine as if it had fallen asleep.

Vern watched as the foreman charged out of the cage and yelled, "Stop that! Stop that right now!"

The man began to furiously pull at a stuck piece of metal when the foreman yanked him away.

"I'm sorry! I'm sorry!" the man shouted.

"Ring out!" the foreman yelled. "You're fired."

"You can't fire me," the man said. "I gave you silver!"

"I said, you're fired!"

It became quite the scene with the man yelling about his silver and rushing to the cage. He tried to pull open the door when two other foremen gripped his arms and dragged him away.

Suddenly, the chaos of the factory shrunk into a tiny space as the foreman was pointing directly into Vern's face and said, "fix that machine."

23

EDITH

THERE WAS no air flow in the room. Doris didn't allow any of the windows to be opened since the beginning of the strike. Each morning, Edith had to wipe a transferable layer of dust off everything on her desk.

"I thought Sheriff Krieger promised *he* could end this strike," she said.

"Promises, promises," Genevieve replied. "I want a nickel for every promise."

Edith wiped a handkerchief over her grandmother's picture frame. "I'm gonna open the window," she said. "You don't mind, do you?"

"I don't mind," Genevieve replied. "But, when Doris returns, she'll just close it."

She decided to take her chances with Doris and walked to the window. Her view from the third floor showcased the strike. In April, she watched a few hundred pickets march in an orderly fashion, holding picket signs and chanting. A month later, everything was different. There was still a picket line, ordered by an injunction that tried to limit the number of strikers, but now, there was a crowd of thousands flooding the neighborhood lawns and front porches. Fights were common with pickets versus strikebreakers and pickets versus deputies. But she was lucky. The office staff couldn't join the union and, for the most part, the pickets left her alone.

"There he is again," she said.

"Who?" Genevieve asked.

"The man with the megaphone," she replied. "Standing on the truck."

She watched as the man thrust the megaphone back and forth. Each sentence was emphasized with dramatic movements and he was there, every single day, leading the crowd in a daily chant.

"What's the chant today?" Genevieve asked.

Edith flipped the window lock, gripped the frame and opened it a few inches.

"Open the trap and let the rats out!" they shouted.

"I heard that one before," Genevieve said.

Edith felt Genevieve's presence next to her and, now, they were both eyeing the crowd.

"Looks like everyone in town in sympathizing with the pickets," Genevieve added.

The chant became louder. "Open the trap and let the rats out!"

"I guess the injunction didn't work," Edith said.

"Trying to limit the number of *those* pickets?" Genevieve asked. "Good luck."

Edith moved back to her desk. A blank piece of letterhead was waiting in her typewriter. "Why doesn't Mr. Miniger put a stop to all of this?" she asked.

"For starters, he's not here anymore."

"What do you mean he's not here?"

She glanced at her boss's notes. The newly hired workers were missing the Sixty B's by a lot more than the old workers.

"He's working from a hotel," Genevieve replied.

Edith stopped typing and looked at her workmate. She wasn't working either.

"A hotel downtown," Genevieve continued. "And he's hired men to guard his house. And the other managers' houses."

Without warning, Doris stormed into the room.

"Shut that window!" she said.

"We were just getting a breather," Genevieve replied.

"A breather? With those rabble-rousers?"

Edith watched as Doris charged over to the window and positioned her face at the opening. "Shameful to throw away a good job," she said. "Especially, in this day and age!"

Then the window slammed shut.

Although she hated to admit it, Edith agreed with Doris. It *was* shameful to throw away a job. Any job. And, the things they yelled about Mr. Miniger and Mr. Minch were horrible. She didn't like them either, but she certainly wouldn't say those things.

"Those disloyals are gonna be sorry," Doris said. "We've got more tear gas bombs coming. And, to teach them a lesson, I got instructions to order vomiting gas too."

24

VERN

STRANDS of damp hair clung to Vern's forehead and sweat dripped in his eyes. The iron punch press had gobbled up a piece of metal and no matter what he tried, the machine was not letting go of it.

"You said you were experienced," the foreman snarled.

The feeling of the foreman's hot breath on his neck added pressure to his already tensed body. The man had been standing behind him for quite a while ordering him to try this and try that.

Adding more lubricant, Vern jiggled a hand lever.

"Anything?" the foreman asked.

The machine was still.

Gripping a wrench, he yanked and pulled it when a sharp pain ripped through his shoulder causing him to wince and almost cry out. Not wanting to lose his job, he tightened his grip and gave the wrench one more tug. Miraculously, the metal broke free and fell to the floor.

"Now, start 'er up," the foreman demanded.

Rubbing his shoulder, he glanced at the piecework goal, took a deep breath and began to work.

25

CASPER

THEY HAD BEEN STRIKING for over a month, trying to remain compliant with an injunction that told them how many people could be on the factory sidewalk, but streets, yards and the parking lot were crowded and the pickets who were defiant got arrested. But, it seemed these disturbances and chants did little, if anything, to stop Auto-Lite from conducting business as usual.

Casper knew something drastic had to happen. They all knew it. And Charlie planned it. He gathered every picket he could, all the men and women from Auto-Lite and beyond, and told them to spread the word.

"Getting arrested, one by one, is not gonna end the strike," he said. "But overloadin' the system will. They ain't got enough paddy wagons to haul all of us off."

He explained how there was limited space in the jail and courthouse and how they wouldn't be able to handle all the detainees. He said, "Do anything you can to get yourself arrested."

And so, Casper did.

He yanked a few bricks up from Champlain Street, ran over to a parked automobile and smashed its windows. He wasn't arrested right away and had to wait his turn. Charlie and a few important unemployment leaders were the first to be hauled downtown. The loaded paddy wagons raced to the jail, unloaded its passengers and return to the disorder.

Casper had time to pull up more bricks. This time, he joined Hank in throwing them at the factory.

"Hoof," he said. "The pie wagon has returned. Let's make this good."

Bricks flew toward the factory windows.

PART III

The most important word in the language of the working class is solidarity.
~ Harry Bridges

26

CASPER

"This is the judge they were talking about," Charlie whispered.

An intimidating desk was set on a platform, raised a few feet from the ground. It was polished to a high gloss with a flowery, carved border, matching the ornate room. Everything looked noble from the marble columns, tall ceiling and gold embellishments. Everything but the judge. He didn't fit in at all, but the comments Charlie made fit him to a "t".

Casper watched as Mr. Schnorf, one of their attorneys, stood up. Charlie said it was easy to find a lawyer. In fact, he found three. All eager to represent the strikers.

"The Electric Auto-Lite Co.," Mr. Schnorf began, "is violating Section 7(a) of the National Industrial Recovery Act."

His first sentence was met with cheers from the courtroom. The National Industrial Recovery Act of 1933 was a measure put into place in the hopes of propelling the country to an economic recovery.

Casper glanced at the seats behind him; they were filled with the same pickets he shared a jail cell with an hour ago. As planned, a mass number of pickets were arrested and the county jail was so crammed Casper couldn't move. Somehow, a jigsaw puzzle was thrown into a toilet. Then the bowl was kicked over and water was leaking everywhere. The chaotic scene unfolded quickly and they were taken through an underground tunnel to the courthouse. The judge wanted to try the strike leaders first, but the crowd pushed forward, demanding to be heard, everyone at once. And now the room was so crowded there was no standing room left, with an overflow of people filling the corridor.

Casper eyed the judge. It looked like he just woke up and when he tried to place a pipe in his mouth, he poked it into his red nose.

"That act," Mr. Schnorf continued, "guarantees the rights of workers to organize as they desire."

More cheers. Mr. Schnorf could only get a few sentences in at a time, stopping only when the applause became too loud.

The judge called for order in the court, but his slurred words were mostly ignored.

Lawyers on both sides spoke. One side wanting to limit the pickets, the other side saying it was illegal. More order was called and not received. The judge resigned to closing the courtroom doors, despite the stuffy room.

Eventually, Minch was called to the stand. When the judge asked his title, he declared he was the Vice President of the Electric Auto-Lite Co. and added that *he*, and *only* he, was authorized to negotiate with the workers. Soon enough, he admitted his refusal to deal with the union's business agent, Thomas Ramsey.

Mr. Schnorf immediately produced a copy of section 7(a) of the NIRA and said, "Isn't it true that you have violated this section in refusing to deal with Mr. Ramsey?"

Casper and the rest of the courtroom scoffed when Minch said he had no proof Ramsey was the representative of the Auto-Lite employees.

The judge pounded his gavel, calling for order in the court, but no one was listening.

Minch leaned forward and said, "The closed-shop agreement is illegal."

The room quieted.

Casper watched the way the judge nodded in agreement whenever Minch spoke and the way his eyes glanced from the witness box to the prosecuting attorney.

Charlie was finally called to the witness stand and before he went up there, he turned to Casper and whispered, "Watch this."

His buddy walked to the stand. Casper knew what was coming; all the pickets did. Word spread, person to person, but Casper didn't know if Charlie could pull it off.

Climbing into the witness box, Charlie's small frame sunk into a stately chair. When asked how he would plead, Charlie replied, "Your honor, I am guilty. I am breaking that injunction."

There was no collective gasp or shock of admittance. Instead, Charlie slowly looked around the room, took out a handkerchief and wiped his nose. Then he nodded. At that moment, Casper and everyone in the audience stood up and said in unison, "Your honor, if he is guilty, we're all guilty, because we were all there."

The room was electric. People were clapping and cheering and Casper couldn't help but laugh.

"Order! Order!" the judge shouted, but no one sat down and there was no order.

Casper held his arms in the air when he heard the judge say, "Well, I can't put you all in jail. Case dismissed."

The sound of the gavel finally was heard.

PART IV

Nothing counts but pressure, pressure, more pressure, and still more pressure through broad organized aggressive mass action.
~ A. Philip Randolph

27

CASPER

CASPER STOOD at the intersection of Champlain and Elm Streets. A service station, busy before the strike, occupied the southwest corner. He had been inside the quaint brick building several times. It stood at the back of the lot, storing cans of motor oil, batteries and tire tubes. In the front of the building was a large parking lot, cornering the rest of the land. Its sign, *Cities Service Koolmotor*, was shaped like a bell and large enough to be seen blocks away.

Today, the corner was so packed with people Casper couldn't see the parking lot pavement. Champlain Street was crowded, too. Every front yard, front porch and driveway had people standing, watching and waiting, with an overflow of pickets and sympathizers spilling into the side streets. Among the thousands were newspapermen and photographers. The Auto-Lite strike was the best show in town and it was reported that theater attendance had dropped because of it.

"Hey," Hank shouted, "Looks like there's an escort car coming."

Casper looked toward Lagrange Street. Yesterday, they successfully blocked a few of the scabs from getting inside. It was rough and punches were thrown, but the workers did not get in.

It wasn't long before they heard about Minch's anger at the blockade, causing him to hire drivers and have the new workers escorted to the factory.

28

VERN

THE BACK SEAT of the escort car was uncomfortably small. Vern hung his head out the window and tucked his knees into his chest as the other two men sitting with him wiggled for room. They were on Lagrange Street, a block away from Champlain and he could already hear shouting.

The driver had warned them about the entrance and how he was going to drive fast. Vern thought about yesterday and how every window in his car was smashed and the hood had more than a few dents. It happened when he was inside the factory and if it wasn't for the armed deputies escorting them out, he wasn't sure he would've been able to leave.

"Roll up your windows," the driver said.

He placed his hand on the window crank, gulped a bit of fresh air and reluctantly rolled it up.

"Make sure it's completely closed," the driver said. "As tight as it can be."

He gripped the crank again, pulling it upward and sealing off his air supply.

They turned onto Champlain Street and it seemed like overnight the number of people had doubled, again, and spilled further down the street. A narrow pathway, large enough for a car, was formed by sawhorses and deputies.

The car rocked over the uneven brick road, bouncing Vern's head against the window. As Elm Street approached, he leaned forward, looking past the other two men and glanced at the intersection. The parking lot of Koolmotor service station was full of people, more people than the day before, and everyone was shouting at their car.

"Hold on," the driver said.

Vern felt the car thrust forward, pressing him into the backseat. It rattled and shook as they sped toward the factory.

"I'm taking you to the Mulberry entrance," the driver said. "The side door. Two deputies are waiting there."

They raced down the street, passing the office building, then the factory. The driver yanked the steering wheel, causing the car to abruptly turn left onto Mulberry Street. Then they stopped.

An armed deputy rushed to Vern's door and jerked it open, causing Vern to almost fall out.

"Hurry!" the deputy said.

As Vern's feet landed on the sidewalk, he had to dodge a flying stone, then another one. In a frantic rush, he ran inside the building.

29

EDITH

"Ma'am, when we get to the office building, you'll have to wait for a deputy."

Edith was nervous. Her escort drove carefully from her house through downtown, but as soon as they turned onto Champlain Street, he seemed reckless. He said his name was Herman or Herschel. She couldn't quite remember. Startled by his willingness to display a gun, he could've been a gangster with Dillinger, the likes of whom she'd seen in the newspaper. But, he didn't exactly look like a thug. All the same, she thought he probably had a nickname like *Joey Two Toes* or *Frank the Pick*.

Earlier that morning, she wished her grandmother hadn't seen him. The woman begged her to stay home, telling her they would find another way to buy food. Edith tried to assure her, but her trembling voice didn't cooperate.

"Ma'am," the driver said. "Hold on. I'm gonna drive a bit fast."

The office building quickly appeared as they rumbled over the road.

"When you get out," the driver said, "don't listen to the pickets."

She didn't have to get out of the car to hear them and was certain he heard them too. Loud and vicious, their words were hurled through closed windows.

The car halted in front of her building and a deputy opened her door.

"Morning Ma'am," he said.

She tried to nod a pleasant hello and hide her nervousness. But she just couldn't.

His hand was extended to hers and she gladly held his grip. The second her feet touched the sidewalk, he had wrapped his arm around her back, making her practically weightless.

"We must hurry," he said.

She was being rushed toward the building as bottles and rocks zoomed past. Each missile crashed against the company sign that was embedded into the front of the office building.

"Hey lady," someone yelled. "Look this way!"

Unthinkingly, she looked at the voice. Men were standing on the sidewalk and one was holding a big photographer's camera. It was aimed directly at her.

"Care to make a statement to the paper?"

A flash of light burst from the camera bulb turning her vision to white. She felt her body being moved toward the entrance and, in a moment, she was inside, staring at an empty staircase.

The quietness of the space was unsettling.

30

VERN

Sweat was dripping down Vern's temple. Yesterday, the foreman ordered all the windows closed and if it wasn't for a couple of broken ones, they would have no air. His stomach growled as he patted the side of his shirt. A hidden sandwich was tucked away after he learned there was a locker thief. There was no way he was going to complain and had already snuck a bite when the foreman wasn't looking.

"Here come the numbers," someone said.

A manager was approaching the foreman's cage. Picking up a tiny hammer, he walked to a nearby wall and tacked up a chart. On the left-hand side was a list of every worker, along the top were the days of the week and, in the middle, were the production numbers.

Vern didn't have to squint to read anyone's performance. Every number was written in red.

The men on the bench were silent.

Vern thought about his first paycheck and how he expected to be able to buy some meat. Even though he didn't make the Sixty B's, he worked a full week and thought he was supposed to be paid for his time. It wasn't until he looked at the dollar amount that he realized he was only paid when he was physically working the punch press. Then he thought about the first time he heard a brutish scream. He thought someone had been stabbed inside the factory. Then he saw a bloody hand without a finger. He didn't want to admit it but the pickets were right.

Lowering his head, he let out a long sigh.

"Those Sixty B's are impossible," someone whispered.

He looked at the chart again. He knew he was fast and quick. And even if his shoulder *weren't* injured, he was sure he could *never* make those numbers.

31

CASPER

CASPER WAS with Hank and they were on the hunt. The shift just ended and one of the scabs was trying to slip through the crowd unnoticed. They were following the man, zigzagging through a maze of pickets and quickly closing in.

"Stop him!" Casper shouted. "He's a scab!"

That's all he needed to say. The guy was yanked to a stop and punched in his gut just when Casper reached one side of him, Hank on the other.

"We told you to stay home!" Casper shouted.

The scab snarled and spit, twisting to break free.

"If you don't," Hank demanded, "We're gonna fight you. Every. Day."

The man hocked phlegm and was about to spit when Casper cocked his arm and punched him in the nose.

"You should've listened!" Hank shouted.

The man tried to return the punch when, all at once, fists were flying. Casper couldn't tell who was who and had to bob and weave through a sea of arms when a picket clocked a deputy and that paused the chaos.

The stunned patrolman seized the culprit and a handful of other deputies stepped in. Dragging the man to a paddy wagon, the crowd closely followed. As the deputies tossed him into the back, people roared, “Tip it over! Tip it over!”

Within seconds, the vehicle was mobbed. The rear door opened and the picket jumped out, but was seized again by nearby deputies.

“Get the coppers!” someone shouted.

Fists and punches filled the air again, sending bloody victims retreating out of the crowd and trampling over fallen women.

A nearby fight pulled the deputies away and Casper and Hank followed.

Suddenly, a loud bang pierced the air.

People were running in all directions, yelling and screaming.

Instantly, a cloud of blueish white smoke began to blossom.

“It’s tear gas!” someone shouted. “They’re firing tear gas!”

32

EDITH

THE TYPEWRITER DINGED. Edith whizzed the carriage to the next line and eyed her boss's notes. The Sixty B's were the worst she's ever seen and the new workers were losing fingers at a faster rate than ever before. Things weren't getting better; they were getting worse.

She thought about a conversation she had with her grandmother. About fudging the numbers and getting the workers paid. Her boss would never know; he was so preoccupied with Mr. Minch and the strike. Surprisingly, her grandmother agreed to the deception. But as they talked through the details, they decided the plan wouldn't work. Mr. Minch would only increase the numbers for the following week.

"Asking how they're doing is a stupid question," Genevieve said. "But, how are they doing?

"Terrible," Edith replied. "Just terrible."

33

CASPER

CASPER GRIPPED a nail between his teeth as he studied the distance between two houses. The quaint neighborhood had homes close together and the tiny side yard he was standing in was perfect. The tear gas used on them earlier had finally drifted away, but they knew another round was coming soon.

He eyed a tire tube lying on the ground near his feet. Hank had cut it open, stretched it into a line and was standing on the other end.

"This should work," Hank said.

Picking up his end of the tube, Casper headed toward a front porch. Hank was heading the other way. The tube stretched and expanded as each man pulled it in their direction.

"Where's the hammer?" Casper mumbled.

He waited as Joe, with his stumpy hand, dug through a tool box.

"Here," Joe said.

Casper held the tube to a porch column, about chest high.

"Hoof," he said. "About here?"

"Yeah. That'll work."

With a few swings of the hammer, Casper's side was pounded in.

"Let's test it," Lester said.

Moving behind the taut tube, Casper stood with Hank, Lester and Charlie. Each man grabbed a bit of the tire and, carefully, pulled it back. It screeched and strained and stretched.

"It's holding!" Lester said.

"Here, use this."

Casper looked at one of the home owners. He was handing Joe a brick. The pink colors of the clay matched the jumbled patchwork of Joe's healing wound.

"From the count of three," Joe said.

The men waited as he positioned the brick in the center of the stretched tube, laying it gently as if it were a grenade.

"Ok," Casper said. "Here goes nothin'."

All at once, the men counted down.

"Three."

"Two."

"Aim for Miniger's office," Joe said.

"One!"

The brick catapulted high in the air, arching straight toward the office building.

34

EDITH

Edith kept penciling over the same word on her notepad, again and again. Mr. Minch and Sheriff Krieger were standing at one of the windows, discussing the situation.

"How many men will you have available in the morning?" Mr. Minch asked.

"All my own men," the Sheriff replied, "and about twenty-five special deputies."

"Can't you make that fifty specials? We have to take steps to protect our employees. We have over sixteen hundred of 'em," Mr. Minch said. "And you need to make more arrests."

"We'll take care of it," the Sheriff answered.

Edith thought of yesterday and how the employees had to wait an hour after quitting time to leave the building. There seemed to be no safe way out until armed guards formed a line. It surprised her when the sheriff boldly told Mr. Minch he thought Auto-Lite botched the exiting situation.

"If *you* would've acted early enough in the day," Mr. Minch replied, "the crowds wouldn't have gathered. There aren't more than a hundred strikers out there. *You* need to eliminate the communists and unemployment league people. If you did, there wouldn't be any trouble."

"Is that so?" the Sheriff asked. "And, what would *you* have done to handle this?"

Edith watched as the men squared off in front of her.

"If *your* men had been on the job early enough to enforce the injunction," Mr. Minch replied, "this wouldn't have happened. Half those people out there are spectators."

The sheriff shifted his posture, glanced out the window, then said, "Yes. There's no doubt about that."

Mr. Minch had won a point.

"I'd hate to see the militia called out," the Sheriff added.

Edith was stunned to hear them talk about the military and soldiers. She shouldn't be shocked about anything anymore, but it seemed each day another alarming event happened.

The men were deep into their conversation, when the sound of shattering glass caused them to stop. It sounded like a window breaking, somewhere in their building.

"If that's what I think it was," Mr. Minch said, "Sheriff, you've got bigger problems on your hands. If you can't protect our workers, we're gonna call out the militia."

35

CASPER

The shift was about to change. Casper and the other pickets were headed to the factory entrance with a goal of blocking the doors.

36

VERN

VERN WAS ready to run out of the factory. A row of deputies formed a shield from the front door to an escort car and the crowd had been pushed out of the way. The opportunity was small because the pickets kept breaking through the deputies' line and rushing up to the doors. With his head lowered and his eyes fixed on the sidewalk, he and two other workers rushed to the waiting vehicle. Part of Champlain Street was guarded by armed deputies and a row of sawhorses. There was constant ebb and flow of deputies and pickets, surging from one side of the road to the other. As he slid into the back seat, a picket raced to the car and pounded on a window.

"Hold on, men," the driver said. "It's gonna get rough."

Vern watched the picket as the car jerked forward. He had gripped the side mirror, pulling and shouting, jogging alongside the car. Suddenly, the driver slammed on the brakes. Then sped up, leaving the picket in the dust.

The bumpy road made Vern bounce between the two workers, adding more damage to his injured shoulder. He barely felt the pain any more as he eyed the man in the front passenger seat. He was holding a gun high enough for the crowd to see.

They moved along the guarded road. Mobs and mobs of people were pumping their fists and shouting, "Scab! Don't come back!"

As they reached Elm Street, the guarded path was in disarray and, within moments, the car was surrounded.

Vern's pulse raced as he watched hands press and push the windows when suddenly, one side of the car lifted off the ground. Falling into the man next to him, he was immediately jolted back as the car fell back onto the street.

"Tip the car!" people shouted. "Tip the car!"

Frantically, he eyed a door handle, thinking about an impossible escape when the car pitched sharply again. It felt as if they were going over, but the car bounced back, hitting the street with fierce impact.

Finally, they were on the move again, slowly pushing open a pathway when a brick broke through the windshield and landed in the front seat.

"Son of a bitch!" the driver shouted.

The car revved and jolted as the triggerman tapped his gun on the side window and yelled, "Try that again! You'll get a mouthful of lead!"

They were almost to Lagrange Street when they passed a vehicle turned on its side, its underbelly exposed.

"This is gonna happen to you if you come back!" a picket yelled.

The triggerman pointed his gun at the man as they sped forward.

Eventually, Vern could breathe again when they turned onto Lagrange.

37

CASPER

IT WAS EVENING. Earlier in the day, Charlie told the men of Department Two to meet under the soap sign at eight, for a change in plans. Casper took a deep breath as he leaned against the billboard's support pole and looked at the factory. It was glowing in the sunset with jagged broken windows reflecting a twilight like mangled yellow teeth. Striking a match, he watched as the bright flame ignited, and he listened to Charlie speak.

"I've been talking to Ramsey," Charlie said. "If we don't change things up, we're gonna lose this strike."

It was true, they were losing the battle and being played for fools. Auto-Lite was still in control, still producing and still in operation.

He cupped his hands around his mouth and lit a cigarette.

"I heard they have a stockpile of knock-out gas," Hank said.

Casper heard that too. Everyone was talking about it. And, if they didn't take some bold, dramatic action soon, this would all be for nothing.

"What they used today," Lester added, "was only the tip of the iceberg."

Slowly, Casper exhaled his smoke. The toasted flavor lingered over his tongue as he looked at the parking lot before him. Only a month ago, it was filled will cars belonging to the long-standing employees. Now, only two vehicles were there, among a horde of hostile pickets and sympathizers.

"Those sons of bitches," Joe said. "Let's burn this place—"

"We don't want it burned," Charlie interrupted. "We want our jobs again."

As the moon rose, a spirited debate ensued. They discussed the number of unemployed people and the nonexistent jobs. There were only two choices. Either take Auto-Lite as it was or, somehow, force it into a fair and safe company.

"Men," Charlie concluded, "get ready for tomorrow."

Casper inhaled one last puff, then flicked his butt on the ground. Rowdy, howling pickets captured his attention as a man stood on top of a car, waving his fists and pounding his feet, while another was opening the hood and pouring sand over the engine block.

"They're never gonna control *this* crowd tonight," Casper said.

"Don't forget," Charlie added, "bring heavy gloves and handkerchiefs tomorrow. It's gonna be an all out fight."

PART V

The fight is never about grapes or lettuce.
It is always about people.
~ Cesar Chavez

38

VERN

Vern's hands were clammy. As the escort car turned onto Champlain Street, he let go of the window crank. He was moments away from the combative pickets when he saw a row of sawhorses and armed deputies. They had lined the street, keeping the restless crowd corralled behind them and, for the first time in a while, he could see the entire road. It wasn't empty. It was littered with broken bricks as if a careless stonemason scattered his damaged stock over his completed road.

"Quite a commotion last night," the driver said.

Vern already heard about the riot. His brother called him, bright and early, and told him things had gotten way out of hand. The deputies had a hard time controlling the pickets and every time things quieted down, another battle broke out.

"Hang on," the driver said.

Rumbling over the loose bricks, the car careened. As he reached for the seat in front of him, he was tossed against the door, then flung into the worker next to him. If it wasn't for the roof, he probably would've been tossed out.

They were nearing the factory.

The four-story brick building fared better than Vern expected. Although several of the second and third floor windows were broken, the first floor was untouched, shielded by permanent grates.

"Good thing those windows are protected," the driver said. "At least that'll keep the rioters out."

Vern scanned the pickets. The crowd was the biggest he'd seen yet. It was a matter of time before the flimsy sawhorses and useless deputies would be pushed out of the way and the road filled again. As far as he could see, people were everywhere, packed into yards, front porches and side streets. He didn't know exactly what happened last night, but, from the looks of the people, they weren't leaving any time soon.

"I'm droppin' you men off right here," the driver said. "At the front door."

A chant started the moment Vern got out.

"You won't get out tonight!" the pickets yelled. "You won't get out tonight!"

Quickly, he ran inside.

39

EDITH

"Ma'am, see that deputy over there?"

The man Edith's driver was pointing to was the same guard from yesterday.

"Yes," she replied.

"Wait for him."

The escort car was stopped in front of the office building. It was the same routine from yesterday. But even with the additional barricades and the crowd on the other side of the street, she did not feel safe.

The deputy opened her door. His greeting drowned out by a chant.

"You won't get out tonight! You won't get out tonight!"

The moment her foot touched the sidewalk, a stone ricocheted off the car roof. Immediately, she was engulfed by the deputy's arms and pulled against his chest. The sound of bricks hitting the car and the building bombarded her ears as she was moved over uneven ground.

"You won't get out tonight! You won't get out tonight!"

Struggling to see her surroundings, her eyelashes fluttered against his clothes, as she felt herself being whisked toward the office door.

"Watch your feet," the deputy murmured.

She twisted her face, catching a glimpse of the two front steps and debris lying everywhere. A bottle slammed into the door, shattering glass against her shins. The deputies grip tightened as she spotted him reaching for the door handle.

"You won't get out tonight! You won't get out tonight!"

"She's a secretary!" the deputy shouted.

The office door opened, then closed with her inside.

40

CASPER

"THERE IT IS!" Lester shouted.

Casper shielded his eyes from the morning sun and glanced up. The soap billboard held Lester in a lookout perch and his buddy's finger was pointing down Champlain Street.

"It's on Champlain now!" Lester added.

Casper looked down the road. He couldn't see the target because people were moving the barricades and spilling onto the street. Last night's game plan was set into motion and they had plenty of volunteers to help execute it.

"Hoof!" Casper shouted. "Let's go!"

Weaving their way through the crowd, Casper spotted it. A delivery truck.

"There it is," Hank yelled.

Despite being surrounded by pickets, the vehicle was slowly moving and approaching Elm Street. Keeping his eye on the truck, Casper pushed his way through the masses, moving quicker than most people.

"Stop the truck!" Hank yelled.

A group of women forced their way through the mob

and began to pound the truck's panels, rattling the side with their force. When Casper reached it, it was barely moving.

Stepping in front of it, he held out his hands and said, "Back it up, pal!"

The driver anxiously waived him away and moved the truck forward. A beastly grill of heated metal closed in on Casper, but he didn't move. The engine revved, swirling hot sulfurous air around his body, and within seconds, other pickets were standing by his side.

"Back it up!" he repeated.

The truck revved again, but didn't budge.

"We're not moving!" someone shouted.

Casper stared at the driver, wanting to pull him out of his seat and punch him in the face.

"Open your window!" Hank yelled.

The man was fidgeting with something in his lap and Casper watched as Hank grabbed the door handle, climbed onto the running board and placed his face in front of the windshield.

"If that's a gun," Hank said, "you better be ready to use it."

It wasn't a gun because Hank started laughing.

"It's a knife!" Hank shouted. "Bruno's got a knife!"

"Tip it over!" the crowd yelled. "Tip it over!"

Casper ran to the truck's side, placed his hands on the frame and began to push with the other pickets. The truck swayed at first, then started to rock. Suddenly, it pitched sharply and that's when the driver opened his window.

"Stop!" he shouted.

"Then back it up!" Hank replied.

The truck's engine revved again. This time, it moved backward.

"No food's getting in there today," Casper said.

41

VERN

VERN STEPPED onto the factory floor. The punch press machines were on, at least the ones that were still operational, but no one was working them. The bench was empty too, because all the workers were at the windows.

Crossing the room, he sidestepped a broom and glass pile, walked up to a vacant window and positioned his face in front of a broken pane.

The mob was still chanting about holding them hostage and he thought about leaving. But payday was two days away and he was hungry. Smelling lingering tear gas, he covered his nose as he studied the scene below. His vantage point was favorable, giving him a view of pickets on billboards and sympathizers leering from homes. Yesterday's crowd was huge and it didn't seem possible that more people could fit into the area, but there they were. The only empty space was directly in front of the factory, protected by a few remaining barricades and a line of the sheriff's men.

"You won't get out tonight! You won't get out tonight!"

The broken window didn't protect them from the noise and he was tired of hearing it. He scanned the pickets. Finding his brother in the crowd would be impossible. He wanted to believe he wasn't there, but knew he was, along with most of his neighbors. They were probably taking part in the chant and every time he thought it might die out, it was revived by a swell of new voices.

"Hey look," one of the workers said. "There's someone on the pole."

Vern eyed a telephone pole across the street, half expecting to see his brother. Its tree trunk quality offered little footing, but there was a man, about half way up. He spotted another guy on a rooftop and was about to alert the others when a brick came crashing through one of the windows.

All at once, the workers ducked. It flew deep into the room, colliding against a punch press machine and clanking its way to the floor.

"Men," a foreman called, "Gather 'round."

Vern peeled himself away from the spectacle and moved to the center of the room. Everyone had gathered around and it was the first time he was close to the foremen's cage. The desk had stacks papers sprawled upon it and resting on top was a blueprint. He squinted at the drawing, concluding it was of the entire plant, including the office building. The part of the building they were standing in was the front section of a U-shaped structure. The tunnels were on the blueprint, too. He had heard about them, knew they connected the front of the plant to the back, but he had never been in one.

"Minch has a couple of plans," the foreman said. "First, grab those pieces of metal and stack them over there."

Vern followed the invisible line from the foreman's finger to a spot by the bench and under a window.

42

EDITH

THE CURTAINS WERE CLOSED. Edith watched as Genevieve stood next to a window, nudged the curtain open and snuck a peek outside.

"What's happening now?" Edith asked.

"Pandemonium," Genevieve replied. "Same as before."

Edith could hear the rioters chanting the same sentence all morning.

"You won't get out tonight!" they said. "You won't get out tonight!"

Each day, things were getting worse. The latest rumor was about a collection of money, gathered to make bombs and blow up the building. And now, newspaper reporters, from all over the country, had descended upon Toledo, making Auto-Lite the headlines. Her grandmother was worried sick, another addition to the stressful time. The pictures in the newspapers crushed anything positive Edith said and convinced her grandmother she was walking into a death trap.

"I don't like the sound of things," Edith said.

"I don't eith—"

Genevieve was interrupted. Mr. Minch had entered the

room, followed by Sheriff Krieger. Edith no longer had the luxury of hearing approaching footsteps. The noise of the rioters was just too loud.

She watched as they headed over to the window, next to Genevieve.

"Miss," the Sheriff said, "you need to stay away from all these windows."

Edith pulled her desk drawer open, not waiting for Genevieve's response. Quickly and quietly, she removed some of its contents.

"If this plan doesn't work," the Sheriff said to Mr. Minch, "we'll be ready. This floor and the roof. And, of course, the factory."

She glanced up at Mr. Minch, wondering what plan they were talking about. He was yanking open the curtains and boldly standing in front of the window.

"What about the plain clothes deputies?" he asked. "Any more reports?"

"A few," the Sheriff replied. "But these damn Communists keep spotting them and running them out of the area."

Silently, Edith picked up her grandmother's picture, folded the hinged leg and placed it in her drawer.

"Look at that," the Sheriff said, "they tied a rat around one of your new hires."

Mr. Minch scoffed at the pickets until someone in the crowd shouted, "There's Minch!"

The observation was immediately followed by, "Rot in hell, you son of a bitch!" as a brick came crashing through a top window pane.

Edith promptly replaced letterhead and envelopes into her desk, covering her grandmother's picture. Then she closed the drawer.

"Get your men in position," Mr. Minch barked. "And, make *my* plan work."

43

CASPER

A SUDDEN MOVEMENT at the factory entrance caught Casper's attention. The barricades had been pushed back into place and the crowd was, once again, on the other side of the road.

"Hoof!" he said. "Look over there."

The double doors were being propped open.

"Letting the rats out?" Hank asked. "Or they need more fresh air?"

Bright sunlight stopped Casper from getting a clear look inside the building. Keeping his eyes on the open doors, he moved to the edge of the parking lot and stood in front of the crowd. He could see movement on the inside, as if people were rushing around, but no one had stepped out yet.

"Wonder what they're up to," Hank said.

A group of scabs began to appear at the entrance, one by one. Then they came outside, pulling a fire hose. They were tugging it over the sidewalk and onto the road, hastily getting into position. The hose began to swell and wiggle and they tried to hold it into place when, suddenly, it twisted and became uncontrollable. More scabs rushed outside to help, grabbing and taming its actions when a burst of water exploded from its end.

Casper tried to outrun the gushing stream of violent water when it hammered his side, hitting him with a force of a million pounding needles. Scrambling for footing, it pushed him around and knocked him down. As soon as the water came, it left. Stunned, he tried to stand up, but his feet skated over a muddy puddle and his palms slipped out from his body. He flopped and floundered, then somehow managed to stand. Seconds later, he fell again, splashing onto the ground.

The powerful stream shot over his head, waving in one direction, then the other. Back and forth it went. As soon as it headed away from him, he scrambled onto his hands and knees and almost stood up when another forceful gush soaked his side. Digging his toes into a muddy rut, he pushed himself upward and skidded toward a dry sidewalk.

With a shake of his head, he flung his hair out of his eyes and looked at the scene. The hose was in a wild flutter as pickets had snuck up from behind and overtook the hose from the scabs. Water was shooting toward the open doors as deputies and pickets ran inside and, within moments, the water was turned off.

44

EDITH

IT WAS UNSETTLING. Edith barely finished typing a word, let alone a sentence. She had no idea how this could possibly be called *business as usual.* Doris called it 'inconvenient'. And, now, a man was standing by her desk, hovering over her.

"Ma'am," he said. "Can I use your telephone?"

He didn't have to tell her who he was. His dirty glasses, tiny notepad and crafty demeanor said it all, but he announced himself anyway. "I'm a newspaperman," he said. "I need to use your telephone."

He was the latest type of unwanted visitor that barged into their room, along with deputies and Auto-Lite managers. The secretaries' office was on the third floor of the office building and an ideal place to observe the pickets' movements.

Gesturing her okay, she watched as he picked up the handset, cradled it to his ear and flipped his notepad open. The telephone finger plate ticked forward and whirled back as he dialed a number, then another one. She sat back in her chair. He nudged her typewriter from its usual spot, picked up the telephone base and sat on a corner of her desk.

"Bill," he said. "Cecil here. Take this down."

The handset wobbled between his ear and shoulder as he licked his finger and searched his notepad.

"Water hose used against pickets," he said. "Short lived Auto-Lite victory. Pickets wrested the hose away. Crowd still growing. And, restless. Very restless."

"I'll say," Genevieve murmured.

"And, several deputies are on the roof," he added.

45

CASPER

CASPER LET the warm May sun dry his clothes as he watched the fourth-floor windows. For the last half hour, scabs had been appearing in them, then disappearing. From the way they were deliberately monitoring the pickets, he knew another calculated scheme was coming their way.

"You won't get out tonight!" he chanted with the crowd. "You won't get out tonight!"

Waiting and wondering, he kept his eyes on the fourth floor when he spotted a piece of metal. It was poking out through a broken window and looked like a generator coil. Then it disappeared.

"You won't get out tonight! You won't get out tonight!"

Suddenly, the metal piece was back. This time, it was launched from the window and thrown at the crowd.

"Look out!" he yelled.

His voice was lost in the chant as he watched it plummet straight toward a group of women.

"Look out!" he repeated.

Helplessly, he watched it crash down upon a woman's head. Her hands flew to her face. She screamed repeatedly as blood gushed from her cheek and seeped through her fingers.

The chant went silent and the crowd became frantic.

A cluster of people began to surge and crush against him as he felt his body being lifted off the ground and shifted forward. He was moved with the throng and, as he struggled to find his footing, he lost sight of the woman.

The packed group surged again, then receded. Finally, he placed his feet firmly on the ground when he realized he was steps away from the factory and a handful of deputies.

All at once, fists were thrown and billy clubs were swung and Casper was caught in the middle. He bobbed and weaved, when he caught sight of a uniform, cocked his arm back and slugged a deputy in the chin.

Chaos was everywhere. The deputies began to backtrack as the pickets rushed forward and pushed them into the building.

Casper screamed at the factory, pumping his fists into the air, when a barrage of bricks started to pummel the building and shatter the windows like popping firecrackers. Bending down toward the road, he yanked at a street brick, but it was lodged securely into the earth.

"There's bricks at the houses!" someone shouted.

Pushing against the crowd, he ran to the nearest home where people were clawing at brick foundations and digging up stones. He eyed a flower border, already picked over, and grasped a buried brick. Yanking and pulling, he tugged it free as dirt flung into his face, stinging his skin like dirty pellets. As quickly as he got there, he was back in front of the factory. Before he threw the brick, he surprisingly paused, turned toward the office building and said, "This one's for you, Minch!"

46

EDITH

BROKEN GLASS WAS EVERYWHERE. Edith hurriedly brushed a space clear on the floor and crawled underneath her desk. Each time a window pane shattered, roaring applause could be heard from the pickets.

Peeking out from behind her shelter, she glanced at Genevieve's desk. Ankles and shoes were all she could see. At Doris's desk, the woman was hunched over, partially tucked underneath and clearly shaking. She was about to yell to Genevieve when a sheriff's deputy burst into the room and raced over to a window. She watched as he positioned himself, back to the wall, and held a tear gas shotgun to his chest.

Desperately, she tried to see Genevieve's face but couldn't.

The man was peeking outside every few seconds. Then he quickly poked the gun through a broken pane and pulled the trigger.

A loud boom exploded, ringing her ears and rattling everything in the room.

47

CASPER

A WHISTLING projectile hissed through the air, skipping over the road and landing near Casper's feet. Within seconds, white smoke had surrounded him and he couldn't see a thing. The acidic cloud was so dense it created a soundless vacuum the likes of a dream, freezing time and his vision in thick murky smoke.

A violent burn singed his eyes, automatically clamping them shut, and no amount of will power would open them. He was trapped in the cloud as tears pooled in his eye sockets and poured down his cheeks. Blindly, he took a step.

People were yelling and crying and bumping into him, shoving him into an unknown space. Thrusting his arms outward, he swung them back and forth, whacking people as he tried to find a sightless exit. Able to gasp a bit of breathable air, he pushed one eye open and peeked around. The edge of the cloud was near. He ran full force until he was out of it.

A sickening wave began to rumble through his stomach. He bent forward, releasing a fitful vomit. Bile burned his throat as he hacked and coughed and knelt on the ground.

He was spitting the last of the puke when he felt a warm hand touch his back.

"Here," a voice said.

It was Charlie.

Casper felt a damp cloth being pushed into his palm.

"We've got water," Charlie said. "Tilt your head back."

He let his head drop backward and allowed the cool water to flow into his eyes. It poured and poured, soothing the burn.

"Casp! You alright?"

He could hear The Hoof calling him.

"It almost hit you, straight on," Hank said.

The burning was subsiding.

"They're firing more," Hank said. "Let's get you outta the way."

Casper felt two hands reach under his armpits and lift his body off the ground. He was pulled backward with his feet dragging behind, bouncing over the edge of a sidewalk. He tried to take a deep breath, but his chest felt so tight, he could only cough and allow his body to be moved. He was set down on someone's front porch, sitting on their stoop. Warm, concrete steps comforted him as he coughed out the last of the tear gas. Finally, he could fully open his eyes.

The smoke was drifting and swirling and the crowd was regrouping.

Rubbing his eyes, he inhaled a slow breath, letting it circulate in his lungs. Then he exhaled it out. As he recovered, he surveyed the factory, spotting several deputies on the rooftops and Hank and Charlie coming back to him.

"You okay?" Hank asked.

"Yeah," he replied.

He didn't stand up yet, but was breathing normally again.

"The canisters get hot fast," Charlie said. "Got your gloves?"

Casper felt his pockets, locating his gloves.

"Here they come again," Hank said.

Several gas bombs were whizzing toward the pickets, coming from different directions, the factory and office building. Casper stood up and watched as they torpedoed the crowd, one after another. Yanking his gloves tightly over his hands, he spotted one coming his way. Eyeing its projected path, he ran toward it and scooped it up mid bounce. Heat penetrated his gloves as he cocked his arm and threw it back into the factory.

48

VERN

VERN WAS KNEELING underneath one of the factory windows, positioned just below the windowsill. His undershirt was yanked up through his shirt collar, covering his nose and mouth as fans attempted to blow remnants of tear gas back through the broken windows. He lifted his head and peeked outside. A white cloud was hovering just below the windows, concealing the area like dense fog. He was scanning the cloud, watching it swirl and move, when he spotted a shiny, silver canister piercing through it.

"Incoming!" he shouted.

Ducking just in time, it flew straight into the factory, banged against a machine, then dropped to the floor. Slowly, it rolled to a stop.

"It's dead," a foreman said.

Vern looked at the cylindrical object. It was covered with burn marks and its tail, a withering line of smoke, was fizzing out.

49

EDITH

"Bill. Cecil here. Take this down."

Edith was still under her desk. Her hands were shaking as she tried to steady her body in the tight space. Every time she thought there was a lull in the fighting and time to get out, another brick came flying into the room. And now, the newspaperman was back, talking on her telephone and crouched down right next to her. He rushed into the room a few minutes ago, his feet skidding over broken glass, as he hurried to her desk and grabbed the telephone.

"A piece of metal thrown from factory window," he gasped. "Hit a woman picket. Blood gushing from her head. Shouting. Fists thrown."

Each blurted sentence he spoke was followed by a gulp of air. She knew it was bad, but this was the first she heard of such details. And they terrified her.

"Deputies brutally clubbing. Pickets overturned automobiles. And set them on fire."

She stared at the man, thinking she was in a nightmare, as she listened to the horrible events.

"Tear gas. From double barrel shot guns," he said.

"Fired from floors and rooftops. Gas so thick, police and fire cannot get to riot zone."

He was breathless and winded as he continued.

"Crowd running and hiding behind billboards and trees. Bombarding the factory with bricks and burning projectiles. Deputies trying to arrest. Pickets rushed them and pulled prisoners from paddy wagons."

Edith knew she was in a lawless situation that had no foreseeable end. Mr. Miniger was safe, working from a hotel, and unable to concede for the sake of keeping peace.

"And," the newspaperman said, "another delivery of gas is on its way."

50

VERN

VERN LOOKED AROUND THE FACTORY. Everyone had taken cover, either hiding behind punch press machines or huddled at the back of the room. A storm of bricks and stones had been flying into the room at such a rapid pace no one could launch a response. The Auto-Lite plant manager had the building in lockdown and different exit scenarios had been running through his mind when he heard a worker shout, "They got the building surrounded! And all the exits are blocked!"

51

EDITH

EDITH'S FOOT had fallen asleep. Repositioning herself from kneeling to sitting, she let the prickly sensation in her foot run its course. She had been under her desk and ready to leave, waiting for a diversion. The time had come. The deputies were not in the room and it was quieter outside, so she peeked out from underneath her desk. The room was in shambles. The floor was covered in glass and brick chunks and papers were scattered all over the place. Glancing at Genevieve's desk, she spotted her workmate's legs.

"Genevieve," she said. "Can you hear me?"

Anxiously, she waited as her workmate carefully untucked her head and looked her way.

"Sounds like there's a break in the fighting," Edith said. "Let's get outta here."

"Come this way," Genevieve said, motioning her over.

Genevieve's desk was closest to the door and the floor behind it was slightly clearer than the rest of the room.

Edith flicked a piece of glass from her stockings and arranged herself into a crouched stance when a window pane shattered and the rioters cheered.

"Hurry," Genevieve said.

Quickly, she scampered forward, navigating the dangerous floor as another window broke, peppering her head and back with tiny knives. Sprinting the last few steps, she finally dropped down next to Genevieve.

"Doris!" Genevieve yelled. "Come over here!"

Doris was huddled behind her desk, arms wrapped around her legs, head buried in her knees.

"Doris!" Genevieve repeated. "Come over here!"

Edith waited for Doris to move but she didn't.

"Doris!" Edith shouted. "Come over here! Right now!"

No response.

"Doris!" Genevieve shouted. "We've got to get out of here. This is our only chance. Now, get over here!"

She still didn't respond.

Exasperated, Edith said, "I'm gonna go get her."

Genevieve nodded.

The floor to Doris's desk was worse than any other area. Not only were there shards of glass, but whole bricks and splintered window mullions covered a portion of it. Edith hurriedly brushed her hand over the floor, clearing a skinny path as she scurried to Doris.

The distinctive sound of a brick skipping over a desktop and ricocheting into the room made her stoop as close to the floor as she could get.

Finally, she reached Doris.

"You're gonna be okay," she said. "Follow me. We're gonna get outta here.

52

VERN

VERN WAS LISTENING to another worker recount his near escape. The man said he had fled out the back of the factory into the railroad yard and thought he was home free when a railroad detective, an enthusiastic union supporter, caught him. He was given a lecture on the importance of union solidarity and how no workplace would be safe without one. Then the detective marched him back to the building, opened the door and told him to take what's coming to him. The railroad men had formed a union decades ago. Vern knew that and understood the back of the factory was almost as vicious as the front.

He watched as more deputies entered the punch press room, load their shotguns and fire more tear gas.

53

CASPER

ALL DAY LONG, sirens blew and gas canisters were fired at the crowd, over and over. For seven hours, Casper and the pickets retaliated. Hurling bricks and stones was their first line of defense. Then they overturned parked cars and burned them. At some point, the pickets had gained ground and almost got into the plant, but the deputies' bullets, shot at their feet, drove them from the building. Injuries only increased the anarchy as others lit burnable garbage and tossed it through the front doors.

Casper was happy to hear Miniger was so alarmed by the violence that he surrounded his home with a barrier of armed guards. Apparently, aggressive, physical power was the only thing he understood.

Word was spreading that the day shift was ending and everyone needed to gather at the main entrance. Jockeying for position at the front doors, Casper held a handkerchief over his nose and braced for more gas. It was an emotional day with triumphant excitement one moment, then miserable tear gas symptoms the next. He knew there was more to come. But the one thing he knew for sure was the chant had come true and the scabs were successfully blocked from leaving the factory.

54

EDITH

Edith was standing in the hallway with Genevieve, Doris and Sheriff Krieger. They were out of the secretaries' office and standing with a man of the law, but the darkened space offered little protection. The sheriff's flashlight and an exit sign near the stairs were the only sources of light. A minute ago, her boss, Mr. Moore, shut every office door and turned off every light. When Doris protested, he said it was Mr. Minch's orders and that was that.

"I want to leave," Doris said.

"Ma'am, I'm afraid you can't," the Sheriff replied. "The exits are blocked. But someone will be here shortly to escort you to the back of the factory."

"Back of the factory?!" Doris roared. "The factory's not safe. I want to go home. Now."

"It's not possible," the Sheriff replied. "The back of the factory is where you'll be safe."

"Safe?" Doris snapped. "I *know* that factory's not safe. Fingers get chopped off."

Edith thought of the senseless way Doris was finally recognizing the unsafe factory conditions.

"Ma'am," the Sheriff said, "there's over a thousand

workers in this factory and half are women. We're moving almost everybody to the back, fourth floor—"

The sheriff's words were cut off. Mr. Moore was hobbling toward them with a flashlight and calling his name.

"We just got word," Mr. Moore said. "Governor White announced the Ohio National Guard is gonna take charge."

"Good," Genevieve whispered. "Saved by the cavalry."

Even in the dim light, Edith could see the sheriff's arrogant posture.

"But there's a catch," Mr. Moore continued. "He'll only send them if *you* request it in writing."

Edith heard the sheriff's breath, a scoffing blow of hot air.

"That won't be necessary," the Sheriff said. "I'm handling this."

"It's almost dark and you know what happened last night," Mr. Moore replied. "There was lots of violence. Like today. And, night's coming. We've got to—"

"I'm going to speak to the pickets," the Sheriff interrupted. "I'll get them to listen to me. And, then they'll back down."

"They're rioting," Mr. Moore said. "Rioting!"

"Don't you think I know that?" the Sheriff replied.

Edith felt proud of her boss. She could sense something different in him.

"And, we sent a letter," he added.

"To whom?"

"Thomas Ramsey. The union's business agent."

The sheriff scoffed and said, "He's a Bolshevik."

"If he is or not, doesn't matter. We want to talk to him," Mr. Moore replied.

Edith heard the sheriff clearing his throat. Then he said, "Maybe you didn't hear me. I said I'm gonna speak to the pickets and get this resolved once and for all."

55

CASPER

DUSK WAS SETTLING in and street lights were flickering on. Casper stood on Champlain Street, the sawhorses long gone. The crowd was so enormous, they filled over four blocks, crammed into areas previously off limits. A few minutes before, he watched a group of men gather at the base of the office building and unsuccessfully try to pry open basement iron bars covering tiny windows. He thought about how every building in the factory had its first floor protected by some kind of barrier, as if the architect had a premonition.

He eyed the ground. Bricks and stones were everywhere, the ones that didn't reach a window. Reaching around people's legs, he picked up a few fragments and headed toward a wheelbarrow. An eruption of cheers caused him to stop as he spotted a woman, the injured woman from earlier. Her head was bandaged and she was being escorted through the crowd, greeted with applause and salutes.

"Welcome back!" he shouted.

As he reached the wheelbarrow, he opened his arms and let the bricks tumble down.

"You taking it back?" Hank asked.

"Yeah," he replied.

The cart was full. Everyone had been pitching in, restocking ammunition piles scattered in the area. Gripping the handles, he lifted the leg supports and pushed it forward. A pathway opened as he neared the soap billboard. It was almost night and their relaunching pile was replenished. Tipping the cart, he waited for the rocks to tumble out.

"There's the Sheriff!" someone shouted.

He turned and faced the direction everyone was looking, and, sure enough, standing in the factory doorway was the sheriff. He was raising his arms toward the pickets, trying to hush them with his posture. He was met with a chorus of boos and Casper joined in.

Observing the man's movements, Casper noted he did not step outside of the building as he shouted to the pickets.

The crowd answered by throwing bricks at him and Casper's hit him in the calf as he retreated inside.

56

VERN

THE FACTORY WAS PLUNGED into darkness. Vern's eyes adjusted to the only source of light, a halfhearted moon peeking through a cloudy sky and filtering through empty window panes. A shelling of bricks and stones was underway and sniper shots, coming from someone's attic, pushed the workers to the back of the room.

Vern was holding a piece of four-aught wire in his hand as he listened to the howling mob. His pocketknife was sharp, but not as sufficient as a weapon made from robust, vigorous cable. Squinting in the shadowy atmosphere, he brought the wire close to his face.

"Hey, Vern."

It was Floyd, a fellow worker, and the only man there that Vern respected.

"I need to get my toolbox," he said.

Vern looked at the bench. It was against the windows, on the other side of the room. Toolboxes were kept hidden underneath and they would have to navigate, not only incoming projectiles, but a glass-covered floor. Men assigned to push brooms could only make one attempt at a time. The floor was never cleared, but, during a lull in the bombardment, they managed to make a decent relaunching pile.

Digging his knife into the wire's insulation, he peeled and ripped away several strips, exposing raw copper strands. After a few manipulations, he managed to bend the end of the copper into a tightened knob. Giving the air a quick slash, he was satisfied and pocketed the new weapon.

"We could use that layout table, over there. Push it to the bench," Floyd said. "Like a shield."

Vern glanced at the layout table. Its thick wooden top and iron legs would make a perfect cover.

"Okay," he said.

"I think it just started to rain," Floyd added. "That might give us a chance."

He was right. The brick throwing nearly stopped.

"Ready?" Floyd asked.

"Yeah," Vern replied.

Darting to the nearest punch press machine, they paused behind it as a brick crashed through a window. Then they made it to another one. Closing in on the layout table, Vern said, "I'll take the right side."

The brick throwing hadn't started back full force, but a few stones were coming in. Hunching down, they sprinted to their target and shimmied underneath it. Vern gripped the edge of the thick wood and nodded to Floyd. The heavy table tilted forward and dropped to the floor. Vern's shoulder was in pain. They began to push the weighty piece. But it was grinding over glass shards and hardly moving.

A man with a broom made a sudden appearance, dashing in front of them and clearing part of the floor.

Pushing again, the table slid easier than before and eventually bumped into the bench.

"A little to the left," Floyd said.

Vern grabbed his edge and pulled it to the left. Moonlight appeared again, brightening the darkened space with a ghostlike blue. He waited and watched as Floyd grabbed his toolbox and placed it between them.

Quickly, they pulled the table back.

57

EDITH

"Where is that escort?" Doris hissed.

Edith was worried too. They had been waiting in the dark hallway for quite a while. The sheriff promised someone would take them to the back of the factory with the other workers, but no one showed up yet.

"I think they forgot about us," Doris added.

Edith looked at the exit sign, their only light. It was a tiny red orb indicating nearby stairs that led outside and the covered walkway that led to the factory.

"We can't wait here all night," Genevieve said.

"What are we supposed to do?" Doris asked. "Go out the front door?"

"Maybe we should find Mr. Moore," Edith said. "He'll know what to do."

"Or anyone for that matter," Genevieve added.

"How?" Doris asked. "I can't see a thing."

Edith squinted and struggled to see down the hallway. "I'm gonna feel my way," she said. Raising her hands, she shuffled toward a wall until she felt the flat surface.

"We'll all go together," Genevieve said.

Edith felt someone behind her. Then an icy hand thumped her back.

"Oh, you're right here," Doris whispered. "I'm gonna put my hand on your shoulder."

"And, I'm gonna put *my* hand on *your* shoulder," Genevieve added.

Carefully, Edith tiptoed forward, sliding her hand over the wall as she moved. She knew their office was the first room and, eventually, found the doorframe. The door was closed and a loud bang from a tear gas shotgun made her pass by.

"Oh dear," Doris said. "Our poor office."

Edith continued down the hall knowing the corner was near. Reaching out, she announced, "We're gonna turn right."

"It's so dark," Doris cried. "How can you see anything?"

"I can't," Edith replied. "I'm feeling for things and I think I just found Mr. Moore's office."

"Is he in there?" Doris whispered.

Edith placed her ear to the door and said, "I'll see if I can hear him."

"Just open it," Genevieve said.

Her hand roamed over the closed door, bumping into the doorknob. Cracking the door open, she peeked inside, letting a dampness seep into the hall.

"Anything?" Doris asked.

She opened the door wider to an empty room with drizzly rain coming through broken windows and siren lights flickering off the walls.

"Where is everybody?" Doris asked.

"Well," Genevieve replied, "We know the pickets are still outside. Even in the rain."

Edith didn't have to see the rioters to know they were there; she could hear them. Pulling the door, she asked, "Should I shut it or leave it open?"

"Leave it open," Genevieve replied. "At least it gives us some light."

They continued down the hall.

"I hear voices," Genevieve whispered. "Has to be coming from Mr. Minch's office."

Edith was tiptoeing to the next closed door.

"We got word from Ramsey."

It was Mr. Moore. She was happy to hear his voice until she heard another man speaking and the rest of the conversation.

"Didn't take but thirty minutes to get his response," the man said. "He said they are demanding a complete shutdown until an agreement is reached."

"And if we don't?"

That voice belonged to Mr. Minch.

"If we don't," Mr. Moore replied, "the strikers said they will enter the plant within the hour."

Enter the plant within the hour?

Edith felt her breath stop and Doris's hand tighten.

"You've got to convince Krieger to call the Governor," the man continued. "To request the National Guard. We're fielding calls from other manufacturing companies telling us to settle before someone gets killed."

"And, there's one more thing," Mr. Moore added. "Ramsey's letter, the union's response letter. It's—"

"It's what?" Mr. Minch barked.

"It's written on *our* company letterhead."

"What do you mean, *our company letterhead*," Mr. Minch asked. "He doesn't work for us. How would he get our letterhead?"

"I don't know," Mr. Moore replied. "All I know is he wrote his response on our letterhead. Clearly to send us a message."

58

CASPER

Casper was surprised by the sympathizers. Despite the rain and endless gas bombs, more people kept showing up. They encouraged the pickets to stand strong and assisted in every battle. He knew he shouldn't be surprised, given the past few years with a banking crisis, financial collapse and shortage of jobs. Toledo had been through a lot and saying things had been brutal would be an understatement. He knew people felt hopeless. He did too. The thing that surprised him the most was knowing these people were hungry and broke and could easily take his job.

Earlier in the day, a sympathizing housewife offered him a piece of pie. She told him her husband was somewhere in the crowd and had lost his job when he got sick. Her eyes were so full of faith, something he hadn't seen in a while, that the next few bricks he threw made it to the fourth floor.

When word surfaced that Auto-Lite was ready to talk, the crowd answered by pushing a car close to the factory, turning it on its side and setting it on fire. A half hour later, when the rain stopped, Casper was talking to the men of Department Two about the union's response.

"Ramsey's doubling down," Charlie said. "He

demanded a complete factory shutdown until an agreement is reached."

"Minch is *never* gonna agree to shut down," Hank replied.

"Ramsey told 'em if they don't," Charlie continued, "we're gonna enter the plant within the hour."

Casper thought about the permanent window grates on the first floor and how a few pickets chained them to an automobile bumper and partially pried them open.

59

EDITH

They did not go into Mr. Minch's office. Instead, they returned to the exit sign. Tear gas had been steadily seeping into the hallway causing Edith's eyes to burn and water.

"Use your scarf," Genevieve choked.

Edith hooked a finger around silky fabric and quickly untied her scarf. Jumbling the fabric into a ball, she pressed it to her face letting perfume smother gas.

"We've got to get outta here," Genevieve said. Her muffled voice was unclear, but Edith knew exactly what she was saying.

"No!" Doris cried. "We've got to wait for the Sheriff."

"Doris," Genevieve snapped. "No one's coming."

"But maybe they are," Doris replied.

"You heard what they said about breaking into the plant within the hour," Genevieve said. "Now, let's think. They were planning on taking us to the back."

"I heard there's tunnels," Edith said, "from the front of the factory to the back. Do either of you know where they are?"

"How would I know?" Doris replied. "I never go back there."

"I don't know either," Genevieve added, "but we certainly cannot go out the front door."

"Maybe we can telephone a *different* taxicab company," Doris said.

When they left Mr. Minch's door, they slipped back into the empty office and used the telephone. A taxi operator laughed when they said they needed a ride from Auto-Lite. He advised them to get out of the factory, walk to Lagrange Street and maybe, just maybe, they could get a ride from someone out there. Even Doris knew leaving was impossible and when they were about to call their loved ones, stones came flying through the windows.

"You heard what he said, a taxi can't make it to us," Genevieve said. "If fire trucks can't get here, how in the world is a taxicab gonna get in?"

"I remember on my first day here," Edith said. "Jean Ann told me the plant is shaped like a U. The bottom of the U is along Mulberry."

"That's right," Genevieve said. "So the left side of the U would be on Champlain Street."

"Why are we talking about letters?" Doris asked. "Shouldn't we be talking about how to get outta here?"

"We're trying to figure it out now," Genevieve replied. "We just don't know where those darn tunnels are."

Edith looked at the glowing exit sign and said, "But we do know where the covered walkway is."

"What?" Doris cried. "No, we're not going through that. That goes straight to the factory floor."

60

VERN

Vern peeked his head up. His nose touched the bottom of the window frame as he looked outside. The night sky had been raining intermittently, but that didn't stop the stone throwing. He scanned the pickets, looking for unusual activity, but the glow from street lights only made the area look darker. He thought about a sniper's gunfire, spotted earlier, coming from an attic around Mulberry. Then he thought about a pickup truck that stopped on Champlain Street with a bed full of bricks. Now, he was eyeing a man on a billboard when he spotted a large drum-like object being pushed through the crowd. It was being moved to the middle of the parking lot and turned upright.

"They're up to somethin'," he yelled. "Looks like a barrel."

He watched as the pickets fiddled with the object and attached it to a cord. A moment later, a large, bright light flickered on. It was aimed toward the building.

"They've got a spotlight," he yelled.

It swooped left, then right.

He ducked down.

"They're using it to scan our windows."

Cautiously, he lifted his head again. The spotlight was aimed toward the first floor, giving him a chance to use the light and survey other areas. Movement at the gate, between the office building and factory, caught his attention. Earlier, he was told every entrance was battened down, closed and locked, and now, men were ramming the gate.

"They've got a battering ram," he yelled. "At the front gate."

He looked again.

"The gate is holding!" he shouted.

Inside the room, he heard someone calling his name. He looked toward the voice and saw Floyd. He was behind a nearby punch press machine, trying to get his attention.

"Use this to knock the light out," Floyd said.

Vern waited as Floyd slid a large brick across the floor. It bowled smaller stones and glass out of its way and stopped just short of his reach. Dashing out, he grabbed the brick and returned to his post.

The spotlight was blazing over the building.

He watched it swoop back and forth when, suddenly, it stopped on his face. Blinded, he ducked down and waited to see if a barrage of bricks would ensue.

Nothing happened.

He waited a few seconds longer. Then stood up, took aim and launched the brick.

It fell short of his target, knocking down one of the pickets.

"Send me another one," he shouted.

Another brick slid toward his feet. This time, he took a deep breath, carefully aimed and threw it toward the light.

The spotlight shattered and darkening the night.

Within seconds, an onslaught of bricks came flying through the windows.

61

EDITH

"There are two windows in there," Genevieve said. "But I think they're both broken."

Edith looked past her workmate into the covered walkway. It was a dark tunnel with a smoky moonbeam slicing the atmosphere. Every few minutes, the elevated structure rattled and shook from a stone hitting the metal exterior.

"I can't go through there," Doris said.

"It's not that far," Genevieve replied. "We'll be at the other side before you know it."

"I think I'm gonna be sick," Doris said.

"Just keep your scarf over your mouth," Genevieve replied. "You'll be fine."

The walkway rattled again.

"Let's go one at a time," Genevieve added.

Edith watched as her workmate placed a hand on the wall and began to slink forward. Her body was crouched as she slipped past the moonbeam, then disappeared on the other side.

"You're next," Edith said.

Doris didn't move.

"Doris, go on," she urged.

A volley of gunshots could be heard.

"They're shooting!" Genevieve shouted. "Hurry!"

Doris bent over and threw up.

"Oh, Doris," Edith murmured. "You'll be okay. But you have to get to the other side."

She tried to push her forward, but she was heavy and resisting.

"Where are you guys?" Genevieve shouted. "I need help opening this door!"

"Come on, Doris," Edith said. "We've got to move!"

"I can't," Doris said. "I feel sick."

She reached under Doris's arm pit and lifted with all her might. Slowly, Doris began to walk.

"Keep your head down," Edith said.

Doris didn't lower her head.

"You have to duck under this window," she added.

Doris was about to walk right through the moonbeam when Edith yanked her to a stop.

"You have to keep your head down," she repeated.

She placed her hand on Doris's neck, pushed her downward, then pulled her past the first window and the second one.

"Come on," Genevieve said. "Help me with this door. I can't get it to open."

62

CASPER

The crowd had threatened to cut hoses and equipment on the fire trucks if they got any closer to the factory. Blocked at both ends on Champlain Street, the engine's flashing red lights and shrieking sirens saturated the night sky with a foreboding, ominous mood. Earlier, the goal of breaking into the building was defeated, and now, the pickets were launching a fire attack.

Casper watched as the deputies raced from entrance to entrance, pumping hand extinguishers over flaming boards. Each small fire was doused in a fury as more oil soaked boards were launched.

"Let the building burn!" the pickets chanted. "Let the building burn!"

"Here," Hank said.

Casper grabbed a board from his buddy and waited for it to ignite. As the flame sparked, he aimed at the third floor and hurled it through a broken window.

"Let the building burn," he said.

For the last hour, that was the frenzied chant.

They were making progress with the fires until a tear gas canister whizzed over his head.

He eyed the flying bomb, watching it head toward a house. He had scooped up several canisters throughout the day and threw them back into the factory, but this one landed on the roof of a backyard shed.

Another bomb was launched and coming his way.

He didn't need to put his gloves on because another picket had already caught it and threw it back toward the factory.

63

VERN

SMALL CRACKLING fires were being doused in the darkened factory and the metal plate in Vern's hand was warm. Extinguishers had long been emptied and, although he could hear sirens, he knew fire trucks had been blocked from helping. Fear stirred his adrenaline, pushing away exhaustion and as he listened to the howling crowd and rifle shots, more glass was shattered.

Another fireball flew into the room.

It split midair, sizzling and dropping to the ground as he raced over to it. Throwing the metal on the fractured wood, he bent down and pressed the plate to the floor. Flames licked over the edges, singeing his knuckles, as he waited for the fire to extinguish. A ricocheting bullet pinged against a nearby machine as a deputy fired a gas shotgun, momentarily brightening the space with its flare.

Lifting the hot metal, he eyed the dying fire and called to a nearby worker. The man rushed over with a bucket and saturated the ember with water. Quickly, Vern flung the piece across the floor, watching it slide toward a growing pile.

As he began to stand, a breeze swirled around him,

bringing a whiff of tear gas. A sickening coughing fit attacked his lungs and his eyes started to burn.

"You!" a foreman yelled. "To the back!"

Vern didn't have to see the man to know he was talking to him. Earlier, they arranged a recovery space in the Model Department, where cafeteria milk was brought in and poured over burning eyes.

"Take over for him," the foreman shouted.

Squinting through tears, Vern spotted another worker, rags in hand, rushing over to the metal plate.

Vern's chest felt tight and his throat burned as he gasped for air. Someone was helping him to the back of the room and leaned him against a machine. A wet cloth was placed over his face and pressed into his eyes.

"Get him some milk!" the foreman barked.

"The cafeteria's empty," someone replied.

64

CASPER

A BRIGHT LIGHT was beaming down from the factory fourth floor, roving over the parking lot.

"It's some kinda spotlight," Hank said.

The men of Department Two had gathered under the soap billboard, setting a game plan for tomorrow. Casper was leaning against the sign post, smoking a cigarette and thinking of his bed when Charlie said, "Casp, knock it out."

He was the best outfielder around and his aim had been dead on all day, but launching a brick four floors up took a lot of energy.

Pickets nearby started to clap. Then they began an encouraging chant.

"Break the light, Casp!" they yelled. "Break the light."

Stubbing out his smoke, he stood upright and moved into the crowd. Supportive hands slapped his back and a large stone was placed in his hand.

"Break the light, Casp! Break the light!"

His stance widened as he placed one foot in front of the other. A circular void opened around him, giving him plenty of room.

"Break the light, Casp! Break the light!"

The words boomed in his head as he held one hand up, blocking the light with his palm. This could be his last hurrah for the night and he wanted to make it good. Grinding his stance firmly into the ground, he closed one eye, cocked his arm back and let it sail.

Suddenly, glass shattered, the night darkened and the crowd erupted.

65

EDITH

EDITH WAITED as Genevieve pushed and pulled at the doorknob.

"Is it locked?" she asked.

"No," Genevieve replied. "The lock's right here. And, it's unlocked. See?"

She watched as her workmate flipped the deadbolt one way, then the other.

"Here, let me try," Edith said.

Slipping in front of Genevieve, she turned the doorknob and pulled, then said, "Its stuck"

"I know," Genevieve replied.

"Can you hurry up?" Doris cried. "I don't feel good."

Planting her feet, Edith gripped the doorknob and jiggled it back and forth, and up and down. Nothing happened. She gave it a sharp yank and tugged it upward, pulling and pulling, when it whooshed open and sent her tumbling into Genevieve.

Bursting from the room was a frenzied scene. Deputies were firing gas guns through broken windows while sweating workers were racing to and from flaming meteors. She watched in astonishment as their feet skidded wildly over shattered glass while dodging a bombardment of flying debris. Their only shelter seemed to be the big machines, lit by moonlight.

"Oh my!" Doris cried. "I'm not going in there!"

"Where else can we go?" Genevieve asked. "We can't turn around."

"Genevieve," Edith said. "I agree with Doris. It's too dangerous."

"What are we gonna do?" Genevieve asked. "Wait for the pickets to break in and attack us?"

"Why didn't Mr. Miniger just give them what they wanted?" Doris hissed.

"You're the one who ordered the tear gas!" Genevieve replied. "Remember?"

That silenced Doris.

"Listen," Genevieve said. "We have to make it to *that* door, over *there*."

Edith squinted at the back of the room, trying to see through smoke and turmoil. "Where?" she asked.

"The other side of the room," Genevieve replied. "I saw the door closing a minute ago."

"I don't think I can do it," Doris said. "I think I'm gonna take my chances with the pickets."

"Are you crazy?" Edith asked. "They'll skin us alive."

"We can't just hope the pickets don't find us," Genevieve said. "Follow me and stay low. And, against the wall."

Edith waited as Genevieve adjusted her skirt, squatted down and scurried into the room.

"You're next," she said.

Doris squatted down and scampered off behind Genevieve. Edith followed as they darted from shadow to shadow, avoiding as much glass as they could. Passing a row of lockers, they had to stand up, hop over a brick pile, run around a man lying on the floor, and dart across the back of the room.

Finally, they reached the door.

66

CASPER

Casper was tired and hungry. It was after midnight and he was ready to go home when headlights appeared at the corner of Champlain and Lagrange Streets. The vehicle was traveling fast, barreling down the road and causing people to dive from its path.

"Get outta the way!" Casper screamed.

Armed deputies were pulling open the gate and it was heading straight toward it.

"It's a food truck!" someone shouted. "Stop it!"

But it was too late. Coming at full speed, it roared into the factory side yard and disappeared as the gates shut.

67

EDITH

EDITH WAS in the dimly lit Planning Department with Genevieve, Doris and the other workers. Finding the room wasn't easy because the entire plant was plunged into darkness. They had to go through a labyrinth of shadowy hallways and mysterious stairwells, retracing their steps more than once, until they accidentally bumped into a man guarding the door. After a frightful few words, they realized he was one of them.

The Planning Department was on the fourth floor, located at the back of the factory and overlooking the railroad yard. The room was huge with a few candles for light. Most people were sitting on desks or leaning against the walls and a few were on their knees, praying.

Edith stood next to Genevieve, listening to a hushed conversation with a manager. He was telling them about the depleted cafeteria and blocked food trucks. He said they were trying something different, but he wasn't sure it was going to work. He talked about the latest rumors of dynamite and goons from Detroit. He said people were scared and tired and begging for food. But the thing he said *he* wanted most was a cigarette.

"Do you have one?" he asked.

"No," Genevieve replied.

"How's about you?"

Edith didn't smoke and shook her head. "Do the telephones work?" she asked.

"Everything's been shut down," he replied.

"Then how are we gonna get outta here?" Doris asked.

He quietly shushed her and spoke about how to use a chair or lamp as a weapon. He told them if the pickets enter the plant, the guards have orders to shoot. But, if they reached the women, he told them to fight. Doris was about to say something when he handed her a metal ruler and told her to keep it on her *at all times*.

A rhythmic knock sounded from the door.

Edith's pulse quickened as the room went completely silent. She watched two figures rush to the door and slide a file cabinet out of its way.

The door opened.

Mr. Moore was on the other side, shining a flashlight. He motioned at something in the hall and, moments later, a cart with boxes was rolled in.

"Food's arrived," he loudly whispered.

A quiet cheer could be heard.

His flashlight shined through the room, roaming from area to area before coming to a stop on Edith's face.

"Edith!" he said.

She nodded a hello, blocking the light beam with her hand as the cart was wheeled inside. Guided by his flashlight he ordered the cart to stop next to her.

"Girls," he said. "Please distribute this food."

Dented boxes were unloaded and placed on a nearby desk.

"Can you move them to the windows?" Genevieve asked. "So we can see better."

"We'll move them as close as we can," Mr. Moore

replied. "But be careful. They might be watching the windows and you don't want anyone to see you."

Edith followed Genevieve to a desk closer to a window. Cautiously, she snuck a quick peek outside.

"Are they out there?" Genevieve whispered.

"No," she replied. "Just a few men walking around."

"Probably railroad detectives," Genevieve said. "And, they're union men."

"Well, that's good," Doris said. "At least this side's safe."

"Here," Genevieve said.

Edith spotted something shiny in her workmate's hand.

"It's a letter opener," Genevieve added. "Open that box."

"I'll use my ruler," Doris said.

Edith pulled one of the boxes to the edge of the desk. The cloudy night gave way to a moment of moonlight as she sliced through the twine-wrapped box and lifted the lid. Coffee aroma swirled to her nose. She inhaled deeply letting in a moment of peace come into the night.

"Boxed sandwiches are in this one," Genevieve said. "And, apples and pies. What's in yours?"

"Coffee, for sure," Edith replied. "And, cigarettes and cigars. And, playing cards!"

"Milk's in this one," Doris announced.

People had gathered around the desk, waiting anxiously for their portion.

68

CASPER

CASPER COULDN'T REMEMBER who handed him a flaming torch, but he was holding it. It was late, in fact after one in the morning. He wanted to go home, get some sleep and think about all this tomorrow, but another chant broke out and he was the focus again.

"Torch the car! Torch the car!"

The crowd was going strong. It had been a violent day and pickets were still fighting a continuous tear gas assault. Many people had been wounded, hit by bricks or sick from tear gas. It was hard to believe: a month ago, he was walking in an organized picket line.

He looked at the scene. A few minutes ago, a car was tipped over and its roof bashed in. Now, the crowd was wanting to finish it off and burn it to death. He eyed the torch in his hand. It was crackling and lighting up the night sky. He thought about handing it to someone else, knowing they would do as much damage as he would do. Then he looked at the factory and thought about the bench. And, how he didn't get paid to sit by and idly wait for hours to be chosen to work toward the impossible Sixty B's. He thought about Joe's missing fingers and Miniger's fancy car. Then his stomach growled an empty, bottomless hunger that wouldn't be filled because his cupboards were bare.

"Torch the car! Torch the car!"

Looking at the buckled hinged hood, he could see the factory's distorted reflection, but it wasn't distorted. He was seeing it as it really was. Warped, twisted and malformed.

"Torch the car! Torch the car!"

He would be happy to.

Lowering the torch, he pointed it at the open rooftop and shoved it inside.

69

EDITH

EDITH SHIFTED IN HER CHAIR. It was impossible to find a comfortable position at a wooden desk at two in the morning.

"At least she's sleeping," Genevieve whispered.

Edith looked at the end of the desk. Doris was slumped over. Her head was turned and lying flat on the desktop with one arm dangling and the other stretched out.

"She's still got the ruler," Genevieve added. "Ready to attack."

Wrapped in Doris's fingers was the metal ruler given to her as a weapon.

"Are you able to sleep?" Edith whispered.

"Here and there," Genevieve answered. "Can you?"

Edith sat up and looked around the dark room. The enormous space was filled with women from the factory. All sorts of women, from different departments and the production line. She wasn't sure if any of them were sleeping. It was a tense environment knowing the pickets could get in at any moment.

"Not really," she replied. "I keep thinking about the messages. And, wondering if they made it."

Mr. Moore had everyone write down a message to be delivered to a loved one. He said they would be given to the telephone room in the office building. Edith didn't even know there was a telephone room but gladly sent a message.

"I'm sure they made it," Genevieve answered. "Try not to think about it."

"But I know my grandmother is worried sick," Edith whispered.

The thought of her grandmother lying awake, distressed and nervous, was too much for Edith. "Where is the telephone room anyway?" she asked.

"Second floor, in our building," Genevieve replied. "Directly underneath Mr. Minch's office. Why?"

Edith glanced at the door, then looked at her workmate.

"You're not thinking of going there. Are you?" Genevieve asked.

"I need to make sure my grandmother got the message."

"No, you can't go there," her workmate said. "It's too dangerous to even leave this room."

"But she's worried sick and I've got to know the message was delivered."

"Edith, it's *too dangerous*," Genevieve stressed. "You saw how hard it was to get back here. We just have to wait it out."

70

VERN

VERN WOKE to the sound of someone snoring. He didn't remember falling asleep or even lying down, but he did know he was somewhere in the factory. Peeling a damp rag from his face, he opened his eyes. It was dark and shadows were flickering on the ceiling. Pressing his hands to his makeshift bed, he slowly propped himself up. He was on a desktop, in the Model Department, with other workers. And, there was moonlight filtering through unbroken windows.

Swinging his legs off the desk, he stretched his neck.

"Just think, this is what we were making yesterday."

It was Floyd. He was lying on the floor, holding a gadget in his hand.

"Seems like months ago," he added. "Not yesterday."

"What time is it?" Vern asked.

"Not sure."

"Men! Let's go!" a foreman barked. "We need help!"

71

EDITH

EDITH FOUND A TUNNEL. She had to tiptoe through a few hallways, wait for a deputy to finish his cigarette, and sneak down four flights of stairs. Miraculously, a window, at the back of the factory, let in enough light that she could read a sign next to a door marked *Western Tunnel*. She had told Genevieve she was going to the lady's room. And Genevieve told her to take the letter opener.

Cracking open the door, she peeked inside. A small foyer led to a stairwell, lit by a single wall light. She stepped into the empty space, let the door close, and stood as still as she could. A dull, continuous sound hummed in the damp space. Taking a deep breath, she darted down the steps, reaching the passageway within seconds.

The tunnel was cold, with exposed pipes and concrete walls. Gripping the letter opener, she began to run. The sound of her steps caused her to sprint on tiptoes until she reached the other side.

Pounding up the stairs, she carefully opened the exit door to a familiar location, the first floor of the office building. She knew she was at the back and a staircase was close by. Within moments, she was on the second floor.

Two overturned oak tables were positioned in the hallway, blocking a partitioned room. As she approached the tables, she heard womens' voices. A lamp, covered with newspaper, lit the tiny space where a flickering switchboard and two women were sitting. Covering their noses with silk hankies, the women were talking into headsets, plugging switchboard holes and fielding calls.

Edith tried to delicately announce herself without scaring the women. At first, she cleared her throat. Then she said, "Excuse me."

Expecting a startled response, she was surprised when one of the women motioned for her to wait, not even looking her way.

A lull in the telephone circuit didn't seem possible, but eventually, the woman glanced her way.

"Can I get a message to my grandmother?" Edith asked.

The woman expertly jabbed a plug into a hole and pulled another one out as she asked, "Name?"

"Edith Johnson."

She nervously waited as the woman scanned a list of names.

"A call was made," the woman announced.

"Did you speak to my grandmother?" Edith asked. "Is she okay?"

Receiving a quick nod, the woman mouthed the word *Yes* and returned to the switchboard.

Edith wanted to ask another question, but she had lost the woman's attention.

Retracing her steps, she was heading toward the stairs when four armed deputies entered the hall.

"Block all the tunnels," one of the men said. "We've got to keep them from getting to the workers."

Edith forced a hard swallow, thinking of her thwarted escape route back to the Planning Department. Deciding it was best to stay with the telephone women, she headed back to the oak tables.

"Ma'am, what are you doing here?" one of the deputies asked.

"Me?"

Edith didn't know what to say.

"You *cannot* be in this building. Come this way."

He led her to the third floor and told her someone would be there shortly to take her to the back of the factory. Then he left.

She was standing alone under the exit sign, deciding how long to wait, when a strong whiff of tear gas circled her nose. Grabbing at her neck, she realized her scarf was gone and positioned her elbow in front of her face.

The covered walkway was right behind her. She turned around and looked at it. The smoky moonbeam was gone, making the passageway very dark. Quickly, she ran across it and yanked the door open.

The same chaos was in the room with rushing men, flying fires and crashing bricks. A smell of tear gas and camp fires filled the air as she crouched down and shimmied next to the wall. Darting around the lockers, she was about to run to the other side of the room when a man grabbed her.

"Where in God's name are you going?" he shouted.

She could barely breath.

"Lady!" he said. "Get outta here! It's a warzone!"

"I'm trying!" she cried.

His arm wrapped around her as she was moved across the room and set in front of the back door.

"Follow this hallway," he said. "Turn right and go up the stairs. It will take you to the other workers."

She was pushed into the hall.

"Here," he said. "You might need this. Use it like a billy club if someone comes near you."

"I've got this weapon," she said. "It's a letter opener."

"This is four-aught wire," he said. "Its stronger than that metal and will protect you better."

72

CASPER

"It's late," Charlie said. "Spicer's here for the night. Let's get some shuteye."

Casper didn't argue and left.

Trudging around people and debris, he headed up Chestnut Hill, then turned on Dove Lane. The alley's usual lit areas were darkened gaps, and dogs were more lively than normal. Lifting one heavy leg after the other, he turned onto Mulberry Street and was nearing his house when cold droplets pelted his head and shoulders. Then it started to rain.

PART VI

Labor never quits. We never give up the fight, no matter how tough the odds, no matter how long it takes.
~ George Meany

73

ORVILLE

Orville woke to the sound of squeaking brakes. His head rolled forward as he wearily opened his eyes and yawned. His Sergeant was at the front of the bus, barking orders about their weapons. They were told to exit the bus and fix bayonets to the ends of their rifles. His stomach churned.

It was four thirty in the morning. And raining. He hated the feeling of wet, sopping canvas clinging to his skin, but this is what his dad told him a soldier was all about. Hopping off the bus, he skidded over the wet brick road, causing his arms to flutter wildly until his balance was restored. His helmet, a steel trench jobbie, didn't quite fit right and kept falling to one side.

They were ordered into formation and soldiers were bumping into him trying to figure out where they were supposed to stand. Fighting with his chinstrap, he tried to stand as straight as he could while tightening his helmet.

Slowly, his squad formed.

Snapping his bayonet into place, he took a sneak peek at the surrounding area. It was a quaint neighborhood like his own, wooden houses with covered porches and tiny front yards. But it seemed dark, as if street lights were out.

He didn't know what to expect from people who called themselves pickets. The only thing he knew about strikes was what his dad told him and it seemed like they were good people fighting for something. His Sergeant said the pickets had gotten out of control and the strike turned into a riot. That's why the governor ordered them to intervene.

More orders were given and his squad began to move forward. The echoing sound of their footsteps reminded him of the clippity clop of horses.

Concentrating on each step, he thought of the crowd and was sure they were gone. After all, no one would be standing in the rain at four in the morning. They'd be back on the bus in no time and he wouldn't miss his high school graduation.

As he marched along the road, he smelled something funny, like acid, then his eyes started to burn. They had barely moved one block when he spotted a mob of pickets.

74

CASPER

CASPER'S SLEEP WAS INTERRUPTED. His wife had nudged him awake and whispered, "What is that?"

He could barely open his eyes, his pillow felt so soft. But she nudged him again.

"Casp," she said. "Wake up. Do you hear that?"

"Hear what?" he replied.

"*That*," she said.

He laid still and listened for sound.

Clippity clop. Clippity clop.

"Sounds like Clydesdales," he said. "Go back to sleep."

"*Clydesdales?*" she replied. "In our neighborhood?"

All at once, he was wide awake. Throwing the covers from his body, he rushed to the front of his house and spied out a window. Rain glistened on helmets and rifles, as soldiers marched in formation down his street, heading straight to the factory.

PART VII

We have come too far, struggled too long, sacrificed too much and have
too much left to do, to allow that which we have
achieved for the good of all to be swept away without a fight.
And we have not forgotten how to fight.
~ Lane Kirkland

75

EDITH

It was a new day, early in the morning. The overcrowded stairwell Edith was standing in was warm and smelled sour. Other trapped workers were with her and everyone was nervously waiting. Her temples throbbed from lack of sleep, but joy fluttered in her mind as she thought of hugging her grandmother and sipping a cup of coffee.

Wiping her forehead, she whisked away a thin layer of sweat and closed her eyes. Mr. Moore's early morning announcement came to her mind. He had entered the Planning Department and aroused the workers. He said that the National Guard had arrived and an escape plan had been made. Quiet cheers erupted.

She didn't get any sleep all night and, after she returned from the telephone room, she was grateful to find Genevieve dosing off. When her workmate woke, Edith pretended she bumped into someone she knew and that's what took her so long to return. It didn't seem like Genevieve bought her story though.

Now, it was a new day and she was waiting to leave. Another rumor was circulating in the stairwell. People were saying Mr. Minch had a secret plan. Despite the arrangement with Thomas Ramsey, he planned on opening the factory.

"I still can't figure that out."

Edith looked at Doris. Her lipstick was gone and a bobby pin was clinging to a droopy curl.

"What can't you figure out?" Genevieve asked.

"Our letterhead," Doris replied. "Our Auto-Lite letterhead."

"What about it?" Edith asked.

"I want to know how that Ramsey fella, you know, the rabble-rouser. How did he get a sheet of it? He wrote the union's response letter on it and sent it to Mr. Minch. What nerve!"

"Maybe someone broke into our office," Edith said. "Or climbed through one of our windows."

"On a ladder?" Doris asked. "I guess anything's possible with those people. All I know is somebody snuck in and took a sheet."

People began to shuffle down the stairwell.

"Or," Genevieve whispered to Edith, "somebody snuck a sheet out."

Edith looked at her workmate. She had a sly smile on her face. She was about to question her when a man's voice politely told them what to do next.

"Right this way, folks," he said. "To the side yard."

A young man in a soldier's uniform was guiding the group out. He was pointing his palm toward an exit, waving the workers out of the building.

"We've established a military line," he said. "A block away. You're safe now."

"He looks young," Genevieve whispered. "Take away his uniform and he could be in high school."

Edith was still thinking about Genevieve's letterhead comment.

"Single file, please," he said.

As they stepped out the side door, a weary manager greeted them, thanked them and told them to get some sleep.

"Quite a night," Genevieve said to him.

"Over three hundred cars damaged," he replied. "And, more than five hundred gas bombs used."

Edith was about to board the bus and snuck a quick glance at Champlain Street. The pickets had been moved a block away and all that was left on the street was a medley of broken bricks, junk and a burned car.

Moments later, the bus was full and as it pulled out of the side yard, Edith got her first look at the National Guardsmen. They had lined a portion of the road, squad after squad, armed with bayonets and rifles as if they were marching into war. And, around the factory, on each street corner, was a military truck.

"Look at our building," Doris said.

Every window was broken and all the curtains were ripped and dangling in the morning air. On the rooftop was a row of soldiers, pointing their rifles as the bus rolled forward.

"Look at *that*," Genevieve said.

At the intersection of Champlain and Chestnuts Streets was a monstrous looking piece of weaponry, the likes of a cannon. It was pointing up Chestnut Hill and guarded by three young soldiers.

"What a night," Genevieve said. "And, it looks like the day isn't gonna get any better."

76

VERN

VERN LEANED his head against the bus window and fell asleep.

February 1934. First Auto-Lite strike held by Department Two, the Unholy 13. Photo altered for 1934 newspaper printing.

May 24, 1934. Caption on back of photo: "Photo shows police in a hand to hand battle with strikers who stormed the Electric Auto-Lite Co Plant at Toledo trying to gain entrance while 1800 workers, besieged inside the plant, dodged missiles thrown through the windows."

May 24, 1934. Victim of heavy dose of gas.

May 24, 1934. Man struck by gas shell. Leg broken. Photo altered for 1934 newspaper printing.

May 24, 1934. Firehose used on strikers. Photo altered for 1934 newspaper printing.

May 24, 1934. Ohio National Guardsmen advance in strike zone.

May 24, 1934. Caption on back of photo: "Above photo shows troops hurling gas bombs during the battle."

May 24, 1934. Caption on back of photo: "Holding at bay a group of strikers of the Electric Auto-Lite Company."

May 24, 1934. Gas bomb explodes. Photo altered for 1934 newspaper printing.

May 24, 1934. Caption on back of photo: "Above photo shows a machine gun squad on guard before the rioting moved toward the plant."

May 24, 1934. After a struggle, Ohio National Guardsmen arrest striker.

May 24, 1934. Ohio National Guardsmen making arrests.

May 24, 1934. Caption on back of photo: "Soon after this picture was taken, Frank Hubay, 27, wounded striker shown being attended by friends, was dead. He was shot through the neck when National Guardsmen fired into a crowd of brick-throwing rioters near the Electric Auto-Lite Co."

May 24, 1934. Caption on back of photo: "This view of the Electric Auto-Lite plant in Toledo, O. shows guardsmen on patrol the morning after the building was attacked by strikers and sympathizers. Hundreds of windows were broken as the crowd threw bricks in an attempt to dislodge the workers."

May 25, 1934. Caption on back of photo: "Ohio National Guardsmen holding a crowd of strikers at a distance from the Electric Auto-Lite plant."

May 25, 1934. Caption on back of photo: "Crowd of sympathizers and curious spectators were forced to retreat frequently by clouds of tear gas as Ohio National Guardsmen held their position at the strike torn Electric Auto-Lite plant."

May 25, 1934. Caption on back of photo: "The resident of the house in the background was arrested, May 25, after ordering a National Guardsman, on duty protecting the Electric Auto-Lite Company's plant in Toledo, Ohio, from rioting strikers, off the property."

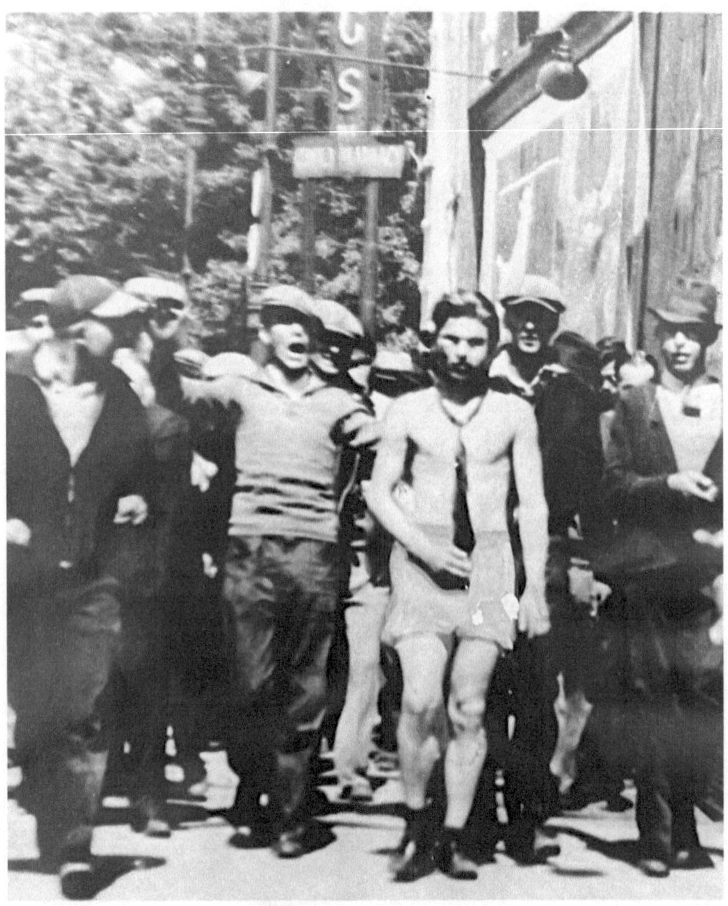

May 25, 1934. Caption on back of photo: "A strikebreaker working in the Auto-Lite Company who was captured by the strikers, beaten and his clothing ripped off him and drove through the streets by strikers until rescued by police." Photo altered for 1934 newspaper printing

May 25, 1934. Caption on back of photo: "Above photo shows Guardsmen hurling tear gas bombs at rioting strikers in one of the nation's bloodiest strikes today as fighting broke out anew."

May 25, 1934. Guardsmen return fire of missiles and rocks.

PART VIII

When I rise it will be with the ranks and not from the ranks.
~ Eugene V. Debs

77

ORVILLE

Orville stood with his fellow guardsmen. His portion of the military line was on Chestnut Street near Dove Lane. They were told they needed to protect the factory from further damage and the military line was established a block and a half away. Browning machine guns were set up at intersections and everyone's orders were clear: do not let anyone cross the line under any circumstances.

Pushing the pickets out of the military zone wasn't as difficult as he expected. He was told to use his bayonet and clear the area. His heavy raincoat and gas mask made the first few jabs quite clumsy. Eventually, he found a way to hold the weapon, poke people in the chest and get them to instantly move out of the way.

Now, he was standing near Dove Lane. The house on the corner reminded him of his parent's home, comfortable and cozy. The whole area looked like his neighborhood with rows of quaint houses and tiny front yards. Everything was inviting except for the agitated crowd and their nasty shouting. If it wasn't for the newspaper coverage, he wasn't sure his dad would believe where he was.

It was a cloudy, cool morning, but prickly sweat was

trickling down his brow and the edge of his gas mask felt damp. Every time he tried to adjust it, it was stuck to his face.

"Does your momma know you're here?"

It was a woman picket, heckling and pointing her finger at him. He wasn't really sure what she meant. After all, he was wearing a uniform. All morning long, taunts like that, scoffing at his youth, had been hurled his way. Not only from her but also from a lot of the pickets. He didn't think any of them could see his face through his gas mask and he wanted to tell them he was eighteen. He also wanted to say they shouldn't be angry and everything could be worked out if they just talked about it.

"Are you scared, little boy?"

She wasn't letting up. His palms were sweating because he was hot, not from her mean words. And that's why his bayonet was shaking.

He took a deep breath. The air inside his mask smelled. It was a familiar stink like cabbage or cheese. He couldn't quite put his finger on it. Shifting his stance, he was waiting to be told what to do next when a stone came flying at him and hit him on the leg. It hurt. He tried not to flinch, but knew he did.

"You're a yellow dog!"

"We've all got our army discharge papers!"

What discharge papers had to do with anything, he did not know.

78

CASPER

Casper was standing with the morning pickets.

"Minch ain't budgin' an inch," Joe said. "He thinks having nine hundred soldiers here, were gonna back down."

"They might dress like soldiers," Hank replied, "but they're boy scouts. Just look at 'em."

Casper eyed the troops. Military raincoats didn't hide their boyish skinniness and oversized helmets and gas masks didn't hide their baby faces either.

"Boys with weapons," Joe added.

Earlier, Casper was the recipient of a bayonet poke to his chest. It didn't puncture his jacket or even hurt. But the gesture easily made him and others in the crowd move to an area between Dove Lane and Ontario Street.

"But they're scared," Casper said. "Those rifles are shakin'."

"Then let's send 'em home to their mammas," Hank replied. "And back to school."

Casper was about to say something when he heard Charlie calling them.

"I just got word!" Charlie shouted. He was weaving his

way through the crowd and approaching the men of Department Two.

"Labor sent a wire," he said.

Casper listened as Charlie told them about the Union's official word. It was a formal protest of the presence of the National Guard. Charlie said that having the soldiers there demonstrated an endorsement of Auto-Lite's position and showed support for the plant's uninterrupted operations. He said it made the pickets look like criminals for wrongly wanting safer working conditions and livable wages. More tension was not the answer.

"Because they're here," Charlie said. "We gotta try to reestablish our picket lines. In front of the factory. We can't let 'em push us around."

79

NICK

It was a cloudy morning. Nick stood at the back of the crowd, taking in the scene. He watched as people parked their cars, one after the other, filling up the side streets and heading toward the spectacle. What he was told about the pickets seemed to be true. A misty rain, brief and cold, wasn't going to prevent these people from showing up.

He was from Cleveland and arrived last night. They told him to get himself to Toledo and Auto-Lite as soon as he could, because there were plenty of opportunities for him. The latest accounts said, since the strike started, over one hundred people were reported wounded and the Auto-Lite Vice President announced that there was over $150,000 in damages to the plant. And now, the National Guard was there.

He was staring at the backs of the pickets and sympathizers, men, women, and children, at the corner of Chestnut and Ontario Streets. It wasn't a great view and opportunities were slim. Scanning the area, he looked behind him for an elevated spot. A house with a banner that read Hang Miniger! Hang Minch! had a crowd on its front porch. A porch that was elevated.

Approaching the building he said, "Pardon me. May I?"

The man hosting the group nodded as Nick stepped onto the front stoop.

The raised vantage point gave him a better view of the neighborhood and intersection. He couldn't see the entire scene, but what he could see was thousands of people. They were packed into a couple of blocks, filling driveways, porches and yards and they looked like ordinary people. But he wanted a view of the soldiers.

The factory was located on Champlain Street, north on Chestnut. He could see straight down the road, but the tops of the soldiers' helmets were the only thing he could see of them.

Hopping off the stoop, he stood at the edge of the crowd. There was a feeling of excitement and agitation and he felt that way too. Reaching into his shoulder bag, he pulled out what he needed, and entered the horde.

People were shoulder to shoulder. He couldn't imagine an easy pathway to the front, and maneuvering the cluster with all his equipment wouldn't be easy. Retracing his steps, he moved out of the crowd and skirted its edge.

Crossing Ontario, he walked further into the neighborhood, going against incoming sympathizers and spectators. Passing house after house, he eyed a driveway with a clear path to an alleyway beyond. Quickly, he darted around a tire swing, entered the backyard, avoided a chained dog and reached the hidden backstreet. Stepping around many puddles, he followed the shouting and finally reached his destination.

Chestnut Street was in front of him. And, it was a perfect opportunity. A vortex of clashing pickets and soldiers, with bayonets and bricks.

He lifted his camera, looked through the view finder, and hoped for a shot that would shock millions.

80

ORVILLE

Orville wasn't sure what happened. One moment, he was listening to his Sergeant yell at the bystanders and warn them of additional tear gas. The next moment, he was defending himself from a mob of rioters who crossed the military line and rushed his position.

Tangled in his cumbersome raincoat, he struggled with his bayonet, then jabbed a picket and ripped his sleeve.

"Hold your position!" his Sergeant barked.

He was trying, but his ankle turned on the uneven road and he almost fell against another soldier.

Hearing a blast from a siren, he ducked down. Earlier, his platoon had been warned about the alarm and what it meant. Peeking at the sky, he eyed a gas bomb as it whizzed over his head. The shiny canister was arcing in the air, then landed in the middle of the crowd. Then another one flew by. And another one and another one. Within seconds, billowing white smoke was everywhere, blooming into a giant gas cloud and obstructing his vision.

"Advance!" his Sergeant shouted.

Gulping stale, rotten air, he fought to see through the smoke as he aimlessly sliced the cloud.

81

NICK

The scene was rapidly changing. Nick removed the used film plate from his camera. It held a riveting shot of the troops advancing through swirling tear gas and he was feeling good. The Toledo assignment gave him a rush, like when he was in France and Belgium, photographing the war. Except the backdrop was different, completely different. It was a working-class neighborhood and the wholesome environment offered a feeling of David versus Goliath.

The gas cloud was dissipating.

Digging through his shoulder bag, he kept his eyes on the action when he spotted a brick flying toward the troops. It hit a soldier squarely in the helmet, knocking it off his head. As it clattered to the street, a boisterous applause erupted from the crowd. The cheers provoked the troops causing them to step forward and swing their bayonets. The people did not disperse or move backward. Instead, they were inching forward, as if the weapons didn't exist. He knew the young soldiers had no idea who they were fighting. They weren't just pickets from a factory in turmoil. Some of them were weathered and seasoned veterans of the Great War.

Tensions were soaring when another siren blasted. Then gas bombs were fired.

Furiously, he dug through his bag, pulled out a blank film plate and tried to hold his ground.

The latest onslaught of gas was working. People were rushing past him and a chaotic calamity was appearing before his eyes.

Steadying his camera, he peered through the view finder. The perspective wasn't good. Backing up a few feet, he looked again. No luck.

A better vantage point was across the street.

He tucked his camera to his chest, kept his head down and darted across the treacherous road. Aiming as quickly as he could, he focused the lens and let the scene unfold. Quaint houses were the perfect background and a gas canister, bouncing on the road and heading toward the crowd, was the perfect foreground. He waited and watched as the bomb skipped over the road, and just as neared the crowd, he pressed the camera shutter, taking an unforgettable picture.

82

CASPER

A DENSE TEAR gas cloud hung over the area, concealing the intersection of Chestnut and Michigan Streets. It was floating, about a foot from the ground and had billowy fringes that were drifting sideways. The only escape was either lying flat and waiting to be trampled or running out of it.

Casper, struggling to breath, was on his hands and knees between two houses. He managed to avoid the thick of it, but his throat and chest felt tight and swallowing a normal swallow wasn't possible. The space he was hiding in was a natural shelter from the gas, a thin slice of yard sandwiched between two buildings. He thought he was alone when he heard coughing. It was another picket, crouched under a window.

"Hey, pal," Casper choked, "You okay?"

The man nodded and coughed as mucus and tears pooled on his face.

"I know how it feels," Casper added. "Just take it easy. You'll feel better in a minute or two."

Placing a hand on one of the houses, Casper steadied himself and stood up. Shallow breaths were slowly giving way to deeper ones, helping to clear his lungs. He was about to leave the safe haven when he had an odd sensation that someone watching him. But it wasn't the other picket. He looked toward the backyard. The space was empty. He looked toward the front yard, but no one was looking his way. Then he looked at one of the houses. His image was reflected in its window, a deep, dark view, and when he looked past his face, he saw someone standing inside.

"Hey you," the picket called. "Help me up, will ya?"

Casper couldn't take his eyes off a terrified woman holding a crying baby. It was distressing and shocking.

"Help me up," the picket repeated. "Let's get out of here."

He glanced at the picket, then back at the woman, but she was gone.

The picket was gone too.

Back on the street, Casper passed wounded people, gashed from bayonets and sick from gas. They were being assisted from the area by others. The air was breathable again. A slight wind helped clear the gassed intersection, dispelling the smoke within minutes. Returning to the action, he joined the other pickets as another brick attack was underway.

83

ORVILLE

ORVILLE STEPPED backward with the other soldiers. Bricks were flying again. The military line had long been dissolved and jabbing at the pickets didn't seem to be working any more. All morning, the troops had been fighting to control the corner of Chestnut and Michigan Streets. As soon as they got control, they lost it. Several bricks had hit him, mostly in the helmet, and his ears were ringing. And, he was sure he had lumps and bruises on his legs. Most of the other soldiers were getting hit too; he even saw a wounded one being carried to the factory.

His Sergeant ordered the pickets and sympathizers to move behind the military line. The demand was repeated at least fifty times, in different ways. But those orders were met with foul, vicious language and more bricks. The line was supposed to be at Michigan and Dove Lane, but it was a struggle just to keep control of the area called Chestnut Hill. Orville wasn't sure what else they could do because the pickets didn't seem to care if they were jabbed. Waiting for the next order, he glanced at his Sergeant.

"Strikers!" his Sergeant yelled, "I repeat. Disperse at once!"

No one left, but a brick skimmed over the top of the man's head.

"Disperse at once!" his Sergeant repeated. "Or be gassed!"

The heckling and shouting reached such a pitch, Orville could no longer hear the ringing in his ears. He eyed his Sergeant and watched the man signal for another round of gas.

84

NICK

Nick pulled a used film plate out of his camera. The four by five glass plate held an undeveloped scene of two soldiers carrying a wounded comrade down Chestnut Hill. He didn't have time to place it in his bag because of an encroaching gas cloud, so he tucked it in his pocket. Guarding the film as he ran, he raced onto a sidewalk and moved away from the gas.

A bombardment of bricks was underway. The pickets were holding their ground and their attack and refusal to disperse caused another round of tear gas. He counted at least fifteen bombs, fired one after the other, launched by a combination of short and long range shotguns. At first, it was impossible for the pickets to maintain their position, and they ran. But they didn't go far. The gas soon shifted, and they were back.

Placing the used film in his bag, he pulled out a blank plate and slid it into his camera. The constant state of flux made choosing a photograph easy yet difficult. His last picture was of the soldiers. The next one he wanted to be of the pickets, and he needed to find a different point of observation.

85

CASPER

Casper was on a corner sidewalk. Another gas bomb assault was underway. People were rushing past him as he planted his feet and let his body be pushed one way, then the other. His gloves were already on and his route planned as bomb after bomb dropped into the middle of the intersection. Holding a handkerchief to his nose, he waited as the first canisters released their toxic smoke fumes.

More bombs were launched and fewer bricks were thrown.

Watching the sky, he caught sight of a canister with an abnormal flight path and it was heading off course. Dashing behind the smoke cloud, he circled around its back, crossed over Michigan Street and stopped in a corner yard.

The canister was whistling through the air and fast approaching. Its smoking tail was sprouting as it neared Michigan Street.

Calculating its projected landing, he tugged at his gloves, glanced at the advancing soldiers, and ran after it.

The bomb hit a sidewalk with a predictable bounce and he scooped it up. An immediate hotness filtered through his glove and, as quickly as he caught it, he hurled it back toward the troops.

86

NICK

NICK FOUND the right vantage point. Close enough to the action but out of the gas. He was standing under a tree, in someone's front yard and it was an ideal spot for another prime, jaw-dropping shot. Partly cloudy skies were giving way to the sun and the tree's branches shielded the light and offered a serene frame for the turbulent conflict. Raising his camera, he peered through the viewfinder, pleased with the border of branches and sidewalk.

In the background was another concentrated smoke cloud, sitting over the embattled crossroads. It was dense and dark on the bottom and white and fluffy on the top. Not wanting to waste a blank film plate, he waited, because years of experience taught him patience and how to use keen intuition.

He thought of taking a picture of a newsreel man, struggling with his heavy equipment, or a fellow photographer, after he was hit with a brick. Then he thought about the homes and fearful faces in their windows. But those shots would have to wait. Right now, he wanted the drama of the moment and an action shot of a picket, something that would impress his audience.

Steadying his camera, he patiently watched the smoke, biding his time when, out of nowhere, a man appeared coming out of a section of the cloud. He was running like an outfielder and holding a smoking canister.

Nick's pulse raced. A knowing exhilaration flooded his mind as he anticipated the precise moment and pressed the shutter.

87

ORVILLE

A SMOKING TEAR gas canister landed close to Orville. His gas mask began to fog as panicky breaths overtook his lungs. Watching the bomb roll closer, he winced and tucked his head to his chest, waiting for it to explode.

"Pick it up and throw it back!" his Sergeant yelled.

He bent over. His bayonet rifle fell forward, bouncing off the street and almost hitting him in the head. Wrestling his weapon under control, he eyed the canister as it popped and sizzled and stopped by his foot.

"Throw it back!" his Sergeant repeated.

Hugging his rifle to his chest, he was about to pick it up when another soldier swooped in and scooped it up.

"Throw it. Throw it!" his Sergeant yelled.

Orville watched as the soldier took a few steps and threw it back at the crowd. It landed at their feet, but they didn't completely scatter, even *after* it released its smoke. If anything, they were becoming more violent and the bricks were coming more often. He didn't know how they could breathe or see. All he knew was they weren't leaving, no matter how many gas bombs were fired. The weather wasn't in the troops' favor either because the dense, smoky clouds quickly vanished or blew back into their faces.

A siren blew again.

He looked up, spotting different sized canisters flying overhead. Watching them land on the street, he realized they also had a different color of smoke.

88

NICK

Nick was in the middle of changing a film plate when he noticed yellow smoke blooming over the intersection.

"Move! Move!" he shouted. "Outta the way!"

He had seen this type of gas before. It was sickening gas and could make people vomit and become nauseous and extremely ill.

"Outta the way!" he repeated. "It'll make you sick!"

He was taking his own advice and racing away from the encroaching gas. Camera in one hand, he pocketed the film as he ran alongside people who were vomiting and crying as they fled. He was on Michigan Street, looking for an escape, when he darted across someone's lawn and hopped onto their front stoop.

Several people were crowded onto the porch, craning their necks for a better view. Every single one of them had a handkerchief to their face, watching with excitement and fear.

"I need to get a picture," he said. "Move."

He had to push his way to the end of the porch, to a corner closest to the fighting. As he leaned against the railing, he slid the film into place and peered through the view finder.

Wind had picked up the cloud, dispersing a dense yellow into a fading, pale smoke.

Shutting one eye, he searched for his next shot when he heard cheering from the pickets. It sounded like a celebration, thunderous and jubilant, and coming from the embattled intersection.

"What's going on?" someone asked.

It seemed as if the pickets had changed direction mid step, and everyone was running toward Chestnut Hill.

Holding his camera to his chest, he flung his leg over the railing, jumped off the porch and took off running.

"They're retreating!" the pickets yelled. "The soldiers are retreating!"

People were passing him by as he tried to steady his bag from hitting his back. Each stride was careful yet quick, and as he approached the intersection, he took a spot on the sidewalk and looked down Chestnut Hill.

The troops were heading into the factory and a frenzied euphoria swept through the crowd. People were letting loose, shelling the retreating soldiers with a hail of bricks.

But it wasn't a retreat.

Fresh troops appeared on Champlain Street and began marching up Chestnut Hill. Their clean helmets and bayonets were shining in the halfhearted sunlight and, as they got closer, a siren blasted.

Bomb after bomb was fired.

Nick steadied his camera, focused on the advancing soldiers and pressed the shutter.

89

CASPER

CASPER WAS HIDING behind a tree trunk, holding brick fragments and trying to catch his breath. The yellow smoke was gone, but an unrelenting bombardment of tear gas was back and people were running to seek shelter. He looked at the closest house, confused on where he was until he saw Lester's wife coming out onto the front porch. Hanky to her face, her other hand was in a fist as she yelled at the soldiers.

"Stay outta my yard!" she shouted. "And go home!"

He watched as she glared down the street, shook her fist again, then went into her house and slammed the door.

He was on Ontario Street, two full blocks from the factory and didn't think the soldiers would venture that far away until he looked toward Chestnut Street. A few of them were coming his way with their bayonets pointed, scouring the area. It seemed as if they were trying to uncover hiding places.

Hurling bricks as he bolted out from his hiding place, he ran down the street and away from them. His pace slowed to a jog as he neared Mulberry Street. Thinking he was in the clear, he began to walk when he felt a sharp poke at his lower back.

"Halt!" a man said. "Or, I'll stab you."

Casper stopped. He didn't turn around, but from the sound of the man's voice, he was still wearing a bulky gas mask.

"Come with me," the man said.

He felt another poke in his back. Then he took off running. Hearing footsteps behind him, he took a hard right on Mulberry Street, cut through Hank's yard, hopped over a wooden fence and darted down Crane Lane.

Glancing over his shoulder, he had successfully lost the soldier.

90

ORVILLE

ORVILLE WAS SITTING on a bench inside the factory, picking at a flavorless lunch. They were ordered to eat, then rest. He was tired, but didn't know how he would fall asleep in the middle of the day. Or where he was supposed to lay down. The place was in shambles. Shattered glass was everywhere and black burn marks covered the floor. They told him the pickets didn't get inside, but he wasn't sure that was true. From the looks of a charred wood pile, he thought someone might have broken in and tried to burn the place down.

"Those rioters are somethin', aren't they? That sure was a lotta gas, wasn't it?"

There was another soldier sitting on the bench with him. A kid from another platoon and he had been trying to talk to Orville for the last five minutes. He was telling him the latest news about one of the Auto-Lite executives, and how the big cheese was served a warrant for maintaining a nuisance in the neighborhood.

"Did you hear what they say about the sickening gas?" he asked.

Orville didn't answer any of the questions, but that didn't matter.

"When a man gets his first whiff of the stuff," the kid continued, "he's afraid he's gonna die. On the next breath, he's afraid he won't."

Orville thought about the statement and looked at his gas mask. It was lying by his feet, like a bug-eyed alien with a tail for a nose.

"You're not gonna wear that anymore, are ya?"

Another question.

Orville looked at him. He was pointing to the gas mask on the floor.

"I'm not gonna wear mine," the kid added. "It's too heavy. Holds me down."

"What about the sickening gas?" Orville asked.

"They're outta that stuff," the kid replied. "It's back to the tear gas now. And that stuff drifts fast. I don't smell it."

"I guess so," Orville replied.

"Plus, we've got back-up now. And they say *more* soldiers are comin' from Lima," he continued. "'Cuz there's word they're expecting more rioting."

91

NICK

Nick wasn't fast enough. He tried to capture an image of a soldier ferreting out a sniper, but the pursuit was gone and all he got was a picture of an empty front porch. Everything was moving fast. A heavy volley of bricks and stones was underway at the infamous intersection of Chestnut and Michigan Streets. Soldiers were returning the bricks as quickly as they landed and both sides had wounded falling from direct hits. He dared to get as close as he could, but, more than once, he had to shield his camera from what he hoped was bad aim. He estimated there must've been over one hundred canisters used already and the day was only half over. It wasn't going to end any time soon. He knew the pickets were never going to retreat. Never. These people had endured so much already.

Orders were shouted to the troops.

Looking through his view finder, he eyed soldiers marching up Chestnut Hill. No longer were they wearing gas masks or raincoats, and they were moving more freely. At the other end of the street was a mob of pickets, standing firm and hurling a new batch of bricks.

A feeling of electricity charged through his veins. This might be the moment he was waiting for. Steadying his camera, he waited for the precise second as the event played out.

92

CASPER

CASPER HELPLESSLY WATCHED. A man was lying near his feet, dying from a rifle shot.

Stunned at how quickly everything had happened, he felt powerless and vulnerable. A second ago he was throwing bricks from a wheelbarrow, hitting soldiers who were jabbing at pickets. The next thing he knew, he heard rifle shots. A rain of rifle shots. Then screaming from a section of the crowd.

He looked toward the noise, spotting wounded, bleeding people when a young man stumbled out of the group. Blood covered his neck and chest and each step he took was slower than the last until he finally collapsed and fell onto the sidewalk.

Screams turned into quietness.

Casper watched in horror as two men rushed to the fallen man's side, turned him over and yelled for a doctor.

No one moved and everything stopped.

He wasn't about to let someone die. Not during *his* strike.

With all his might, he shouted, "Is there a doctor around. We need a doctor over here! Now!"

93

NICK

The area fell silent. No bricks. No stones. No bayonets. Just gas, drifting away.

Nick furiously scanned the intersection looking for the reason. A moment ago, he excitedly photographed a chaotic, clashing scene when he heard rifle shots coming from the soldiers.

The gas was lifting and revealing pickets, wounded and shocked, all looking in the same direction. As quick as he could, he removed the used film plate and followed their gaze to the opposite side of the street.

On the corner were three men, kneeling on a sidewalk.

With a rush of adrenaline, he slid blank film into his camera and examined the scene. But he was too far away.

Keeping his eyes on the corner, he carefully lifted his camera, looked through the view finder and began to cross the intersection. Each step was blindly taken and as he nudged bricks from his path he did not lose sight of the drama.

Suddenly, the image was clear.

The kneeling men were tending to a bloody body.

It was a once-in-a-lifetime shot. Stunned pickets in the

background, dying man in the foreground. And, three men trying to save his life.

He focused his camera, closing in on the rare image, when he accidentally kicked a stone, notifying the men of his presence. They looked up at his camera. Their eyes immediately changed from concern to disgust as he pressed the shutter.

94

CASPER

THE WOUNDED and dead had been carried away by pickets. Casper looked at the wheelbarrow. A few bricks were left, but he didn't want to throw them anymore. There was a pause in the fighting, but a tenseness remained. He thought it might be the end of the strike until he saw a truck driving up Chestnut Hill. Soldier were sitting in its bed and as they drove past, they tossed gas grenades into the crowd.

"They're throwing Dutch Pepper Bombs!" someone yelled.

The gas began to circulate. The pickets moved back.

"Minch doesn't care if we die," Hank said.

"He doesn't," Casper replied. "Not at all."

95

NICK

THE GAS GRENADES did not prompt a retaliation, but more sympathizers were showing up and joining the pickets. The crowd was the largest Nick had seen all day. But they were sullen and quiet. Even the soldiers were standing around, leaning on their rifles or sitting on a curb. It was incredible to believe, but not too long ago, the battle was heated and two men were killed.

He took advantage of the temporary lull and sat down in the grass. Evening was approaching and capturing the events without daylight would no longer be possible. Searching his shoulder bag, he needed to take inventory and opened a padded sack. Safely inside were used film plates. Most of them contained extraordinary scenes and would be developed before tomorrow's newspaper deadline. With a little luck, one might make the front page.

Hungry and out of blank film plates, he picked up his bag and left the area.

96

CASPER

"Let's go home and get some rest," Charlie said. "Lester and Bill are comin' back at eight. They're gonna launch some night operations."

Casper headed home, walking through a new crowd of people. They seemed anxious and keyed up and ready for the night.

PART IX

Injustice boils in men's hearts as does steel in its cauldron, ready to pour forth, white hot, in the fullness of time.
~ Mother Jones

97

ORVILLE

Orville's neck was stiff. He wasn't sure if it was from the wobbly cot or wearing a gas mask all day. Either way, he didn't sleep much. On one side of him, a guy snored like a motor, on the other side, someone was crying about missing a high school graduation. After putting a flimsy pillow on his face, he finally fell asleep. But it didn't last long. Peaceful sleep turned into a fitful rest.

Morning came quickly, or what he thought was morning. They said he slept over six hours and, surprisingly, it was still the same day. The fourth floor of the factory, at the north end, housed the soldiers and the lighting outside could've easily been seven o'clock in the morning, instead of seven o'clock at night.

Groggy, he sat up and swung his legs to the floor. His whole body ached. Bruises and welts covered his legs, some the size of his fist. But, in comparison to the bandaged soldiers along the wall, he had fared quite well. Getting ready was difficult. He didn't want to go outside. No one wanted to be there anymore and everyone was moving slowly.

Soon enough, his platoon was made aware of the most

recent riots. He learned of the two men who died. And, a statement issued by a Colonel that read:

"No orders were issued by any officers for the firing which occurred this afternoon when two men were killed. Apparently, some soldiers injured by flying missiles from the mob, shot over the heads of the crowd to put a stop to the hail of bricks and bottles. This firing probably caused others to open fire, this time into the mob."

He also heard about *another* order. One that said the soldiers *should* fire again if rioters placed their lives in jeopardy. Then they were told preparations were being made for the night and a machine gun had been moved in front of the factory's main gate.

The Vice President of Auto-Lite made an appearance. Orville thought he looked like a mean principal or stingy clergyman, but he paid attention when they were told radicals from nearby cities were on their way to help the pickets riot. And, they were bringing dynamite.

Then quicker than Orville wanted, he was back outside.

It was dusk and the air was acidic, but gas masks were no longer required.

The rioters were still there. Every available space was filled with them. He couldn't see the depth of the crowd, but he could hear them, loud and clear.

"Wait until it gets dark, boys," they chanted. "Wait until it gets dark."

98

SAMMY

Sammy stood in front of a burned Tin Lizzie. He had to push through the evening crowd to get a better look, and now he was staring at a scorched car frame. The fender was marbling and had blisters and flakes. He touched the scarred metal, flinching from the heat.

"Sam!"

It was his buddy, calling him.

"Look at this," Carl said.

A piece of metal, the size a small bat, was in his buddy's hand. It was smooth on one end and jagged on the other.

"This will come in handy," Carl added.

Sammy patted his pocket, confirming a handful of stones, then looked at the car.

"What happened to this iron?" Carl asked.

"Burned," Sammy replied.

All at once, Carl raised his fist, metal in hand, and slammed it into the hood. A dent, the size of a baseball, puckered the hood, like a damaged can of beans.

"Killed," Carl said. "What else is in this area?"

Sammy thought about what he'd already seen: houses

with broken windows and trampled gardens, heaping piles of bricks and stones, and flipped cars.

"Lots of stuff," he replied. "And, there's a service station over there. Let's—"

A burst of cheers interrupted his thought. It was coming from a section of pickets near the factory.

"Come on!" Carl said.

Sammy followed his buddy toward the cheers, shoving people from his path if they didn't move. Eventually, they ended up across the street from a brick building, attached to the factory by a covered walkway. The action was on Chestnut Street.

"Look at 'em," Carl said. "They're retreating."

He watched the soldiers get pummeled by bricks, limping backward down the sloped street. They looked young, about his age, but didn't have his mental strength.

"Cowards!" Sammy shouted.

"Listen to the chant," Carl said.

Sammy tuned in to the pickets.

"Wait until it gets dark boys!" they said. "Wait until it gets dark!"

The last of the day's light reflected on the soldiers' bayonets.

Eyeing their shaking weapons and scared faces, Sammy muttered, "I'll give ya somethin' to be scared about."

Reaching into his pocket, he pulled out a stone and chucked it at the troops.

"Yeah!" he yelled, "Wait till it gets dark!"

99

ORVILLE

ORVILLE DUCKED AND SWERVED, dodging brick after brick, but dusk made it difficult to see. Pulling his rifle close to his chest, he lowered his head, planted his feet and tried not to step backward. Stones and glass were pelting him, ricocheting off his helmet and hitting his body. His thick uniform had protected him from cuts, but bruises from the morning were being hit. He thought about the order of using his rifle, if his life was in jeopardy. He wanted to fire it and stop the abuse, but none of the other soldiers had their rifles aimed.

Orders were given to throw back the bricks and march up Chestnut Hill. But with so many incoming objects all he had time to do was dodge everything.

A siren blasted.

Canister after canister flew overhead and a thick cloud of smoke began to form over the pickets. Suddenly, the bricks stopped.

Breathing a sigh of relief, he watched the gas cloud bloom, then eyed the road. A brick chunk was by his foot. Picking it up, he threw it into the smoke, hoping it hit someone. Then he picked up another brick. And soon, his unit was advancing.

100

LESTER

IT WAS NIGHT. The street lights, those that were not broken, flashed on. A crowd had packed the parking lot at the corner of Champlain and Elm Streets and Lester was in it. He knew men would still be there, but it surprised him to see women and children. Everyone knew they were taking a chance of being gassed or hit or shot. But it seemed no one cared about that. Everyone wanted to see the spectacle.

Standing on the steps to the Koolmotor service station, he was elevated and had a partial view of the factory. Moments ago, the troops had advanced, across Champlain Street and up Chestnut Hill, but an onslaught of bricks quickly drove them backward. Now, they were standing along Champlain Street, like sitting ducks.

"See that lousy chump over there?" Bill asked. "On the end."

Lester eyed the soldier. They all looked alike to him. Young, grim and limping.

"That one?" he asked.

"Yeah," Bill replied. "I clocked him in the knee. And, I could tell it hurt."

"That's good," Lester murmured.

Rubbing a stone in his hand, he glanced at a street lamp. It was attached to a telephone pole and dangling above the troops. Confident in his aim, he said, "I'm gonna knock that light out."

He stepped off the stoop, making an opening in the crowd when he told them what his plans were. Then he took aim and threw the stone. It sailed in the air.

The street light went dark and the globe clattered to the street.

People cheered, then booed as headlights appeared, coming from Lagrange Street. It was a car, slowly advancing toward them and lighting up the road.

Lester bolted around the back of the crowd, took a sharp left through someone's yard, then ran toward the car. He couldn't see inside; the headlights were bright and blinding and giving the troops a view of the pickets.

"What are you doin' here?" he yelled. "Turn off your damn lights!"

The car was surrounded by pickets.

"It's okay," one of the pickets said. "I know him and he's just tryin' to get home."

"Where's he live?" Lester asked.

"Mulberry and Ontario," the picket replied, "next to me. His wife and baby are waiting for him."

"Tell him to turn his lights off!" Lester replied. "And, take Dove Lane."

"Turn your lights off!" the crowd chanted. "Turn your lights off!"

101

SAMMY

"Let's go around back," Carl said.

Sammy followed his buddy to the other side of the Koolmotor service station. It was on a corner and the backyard edged a side street. He glanced at the dark space. It was empty except for a couple of men, smoking and talking.

"Evening," Sammy nodded.

The men didn't notice him so he approached the back of the building. It was a small brick structure with two windows. Cautiously, he moved through the yard and stepped up to the window furthest from the street. Thick glass hid a dark room and didn't give him any idea of the inside. Placing his hands on the frame, he jiggled it.

"Use this," Carl said.

Grabbing the piece of metal from his buddy's hand, he held it like a hammer, glanced at the men, then smashed a pane. A jagged round hole appeared. With a few more whacks, the window was demolished, mullions and all. Pulling his jacket sleeve over his hand, he brushed shards from the frame and hoisted his body upward. As his legs dangled outside, he looked around the dark room, spotting a dimly lit counter on the other side. Then he pulled himself inside.

A tiny flame from his cigarette lighter helped him scan the room. Tire tubes, oil cans, lubricants, and batteries filled a back shelf, and a cluttered counter, with a cash register, was in the front. He made his way to the counter, rifled through the mess on top and pocketed a compression gauge, chocolate bar and a few other trinkets.

"Hey," Carl whispered. "Look at this."

Sammy looked at his buddy. He was shining a flashlight on the back wall where a pay telephone was anchored. His finger was digging in the coin slot.

"Anything?" Sammy asked.

"Nah'," Carl replied.

He watched his buddy try to wiggle the telephone box from the wall. It didn't seem to be moving.

"Give me a hand, will ya?" Carl asked.

He was on his way to help when he stubbed his toe and tripped over something heavy. Pointing the lighter toward his feet, he spotted an oil can oozing onto the floor. Quickly, he pulled the flame away and stood upright.

"Hey, I got it," Carl announced.

Sammy watched as Carl carried the heavy telephone to the window, then disappeared with his haul into the night.

Looking down at the expanding oil spill, he stepped around it and headed back to the cash register.

The lighter flame lit the machine, showcasing a sales window and many buttons. Some had words like gas, oil, grease, and labor and other were just numbers. Pressing a few keys, he hoped to find the right combination, but no bell rang. Using his fist, he thumped the drawer, banging it a few times. Still nothing.

Eyeing his lucky number, he pressed the key, then the motor bar. The drawer shot open with a ding. Although the dollar slots were empty, he pocketed all the coins.

102

LESTER

A LULL in the gas bombing allowed the pickets to regain their ground. Most of the night fighting had been in three spots: the intersection of Chestnut and Michigan, along Elm Street and the vacant Auto-Lite parking lot.

Lester started out on Elm Street with Bill, but after they ran out of bricks, he darted to Champlain Street, wanting to get near the factory. But the crowd was so thick he couldn't reach the fighting. A few unplanned turns, and now he was standing at the crossroads of Chestnut and Michigan, where, at the moment, it was calm.

Surging forward with the crowd, he yelled, "What's the matter? Running out of gas?"

Rhythmic voices started to chant, getting louder and louder.

"Give. Us. Gas!" the pickets shouted. "Give. Us. Gas!"

Lester raised his fists, pounded the air and joined the chant.

103

ORVILLE

Orville was standing on Champlain Street. They hadn't been ordered to advance in a while and all he could hear, besides the pickets, was the popping sounds of stones hitting helmets, including his own.

The rioters were reckless and disrespectful. He didn't respect them either and was sick of it all and wanted to go home.

Relief finally came when a siren blasted and a renewed tear gas attack was launched.

104

SAMMY

RESTRICTED AREAS THRILLED SAMMY. Especially at night, and the railroad coal yard behind the factory was no different. He had jumped a moving train before and considered himself a railroader, but these boxcars were not moving, making them an easy target. Railroad detectives were of no concern, at least for the moment. An *unexpected* fire in the yard pulled them away.

He walked over to a boxcar full of coal, hoisted his leg onto a ladder rung and scurried his way to the top. The boxcar was brimming with coal chunks, glimmering in the moonlight. Hopping onto the rocky surface, he wobbled as he walked, picking up pieces that would fit in his pockets.

Satisfied, he stood upright and surveyed the area. Pole lights dotted the yard and a blaze of orange lit a section near the factory. Grabbing a piece of coal, he threw it at a nearby light, but missed.

"Eh," he said. "You get to live another day."

Swinging his legs over the wall, he hooked a foot onto the ladder, hustled to the last rung and jumped to the ground.

"Hey you!"

The voice startled him. He bolted to a different train, hid behind a boxcar and waited.

105

ORVILLE

THE SOLDIERS COULDN'T HOLD their ground, even with the gas. Orville was back on Champlain Street. His platoon had made it to the top of Chestnut Hill, only to be driven backward by bricks, glass and coal.

News circulated about a fire behind the factory and how fire trucks were blocked as they attempted to extinguish the blaze. Nothing was stopping these rioters. He hoped there was an endless supply of tear gas because they were going to need it.

106

LESTER

IT WAS close to midnight when Lester heard clanking on a nearby roof. One of the tear gas canisters had rolled, then stopped on top of a house.

"It's on the roof!" someone shouted.

All heads turned toward the house. A moment later, the front door flung open. A lady, in a night gown and carrying a toddler, came screaming outside, followed by two other children and an old woman.

Lester recognized the people. They were the family of an Auto-Lite worker.

107

SAMMY

SAMMY MADE it out of the railroad yard after chucking a piece of coal at a railroad detective. It felt good to hit the man, square in his chest, and teach him a lesson on why he shouldn't sneak up on a fellow.

He was making his way to the riot area when he stumbled across a shallow ditch where two pickets were tearing apart an old, wooden footbridge. Each plank was being pried up and tossed into a wheelbarrow.

Picking up a plank, he eyed the nails sticking out of it, marveling at the possibilities, when out of nowhere, a tear gas canister landed next to him. It was smoking and popping, and suddenly burst. Gas instantly clouded the area, sending Sammy bolting to Elm Street.

108

ORVILLE

Orville's unit was being relieved. It was in the middle of the night and things had quieted down. The crowd seemed smaller too, allowing the military line to be reestablished to its original position. Earlier, he had watched a squad of policemen go through the crowd and plead with pickets and sympathizers to leave. Surprisingly, most of the people did, leaving only around six hundred or so left in the area.

He was hungry and tired and the thought of military food and a cot seemed like heaven to him.

109

SAMMY

SAMMY DIDN'T KNOW how Carl found an old ice wagon. He said it was in some alleyway and, with the help of another rioter, he pushed it to the top of Chestnut Hill.

"My grandpa used to have one of these," Carl said. "Just like this one."

Sammy looked at the wagon. Several of its wooden wall panels were missing and its wheels were a bit cockeyed.

"I think it will still roll," Carl added.

Gray streaks of dawn could be seen in the east and Sammy knew this was their last hurrah, at least for *this* night.

"Let's give it a shot," Sammy replied.

The rickety wagon screeched over the road as they aimed it toward the factory.

"Not much of a hill," Carl said. "It'll need a big push."

Sammy placed his hands on the back of the wagon and a few other rioters joined in.

"On the count of three," Carl said. "Ready?"

Digging his feet in, Sammy eyed the others as they nodded.

"One. Two. Three!"

It slowly started to move. Then as they pushed harder, it

took off and rolled down the hill. It was rattling and shaking, as if it was going to completely fall apart, when one of its wheels came off. It veered off course and smashed into a telephone pole.

A tear gas canister bounced up the street, landing near their feet.

Sammy took off running.

PART X

Labor unions were not built by men and women who got their feelings hurt or quit after the first disappointment.
~ Josephine Hoffa

110

ORVILLE

ORVILLE WAS TRYING to be as polite as he could. He woke up with a headache and wasn't in a good mood. It was six thirty in the morning on Friday and workers were showing up, ready to work. Some were allowed inside, to sweep up the floors. Others had to be told the plant was closed and they were to leave.

He followed the orders and told the workers and found it strange when some of them looked familiar. Asking one of the men how they knew one another, he didn't receive an answer. Instead, the man shrugged. Another question asked and the results were the same.

Giving it one more shot, Orville said, "Do you know my dad?"

The man laughed, igniting a flicker of Orville's memory, then igniting betrayal in Orville's heart.

The worker was in last night's crowd. *And* throwing bricks at his squad.

Stunned, Orville could not speak and lost his opportunity to retaliate when the man walked away. They were ordered to protect the workers, keep them safe and unharmed. Maybe his mind was playing tricks on him. A worker wouldn't join the rebellious rioters for a cheap shot, but, then again, the man did have a treasonous look in his eye.

Taking a troubled breath, his thinking ping-ponged as he joined his unit in front of the factory. An update about last night's events was in progress. He listened as his Sergeant told them over fifty strikers and spectators had been arrested, booked at the Safety Building and charged with rioting. They were being informed that scores of armed sympathizers and radical elements were on their way from Chicago, Cleveland and Detroit. Then a statement was read from Mr. Minch, the Vice President of Auto-Lite. He said a private detective agency uncovered a scheme to dynamite the factory.

Four additional companies arrived last night. His Sergeant said they were now part of a battalion of over thirteen hundred soldiers and today's tactics would be aggressive. And every soldier needed to be watchful, assertive and unrelenting.

His head throbbed.

Orders were issued and he began to march up Chestnut Hill.

People were still there, just not as many. Only numbering in the hundreds. It was the smallest crowd he'd seen since his arrival and they weren't combative, at least at the moment. They said the cold wind kept most of the bastards away. Probably tucked in a warm bed.

More orders were barked. The day's plan was set and he was told to be ready for the aggressive offense. He was ready. Ready to go home.

111

NICK

"THIS IS as close as I can get," the cabbie said.

Nick eyed the corner of Lagrange and Champlain Streets. The riot area was blocked to vehicle traffic, barred by a row of sawhorses on Champlain and forcing a line of illegally parked cars along Lagrange.

The noon hour, a late start for him, made him feel anxious. His hotel was packed and his breakfast was late, then the doorman had a line of people waiting for cabs. Everyone was going to the same place, he was positive about that, but when he tried to share another photographer's cab, the door closed on him.

The traffic offered one positive note: it seemed that everyone had waited for the morning wind to die out.

Dropping a few coins into the cabbie's palm, he grabbed his shoulder bag, opened the door and swung his leg outside. Lively voices, movement and energy filled the streets and, everywhere he looked, people were coming into the neighborhood.

"Thanks for the lift," he said.

Getting out of the car, he was thinking about his plan and was about to join the pickets when he spotted a wild-eyed man making a break from the crowd. His arms were pumping and his legs were sprinting and he was heading straight toward Nick's cab.

Before he knew it, the man had dived through the opened door and was breathlessly yelling a street address. As he tugged at the door, Nick tried to free his trapped bag and the delayed departure allowed the pickets to catch up.

"Get that scab!" they yelled. "Come out and take what's comin' to ya!"

The taxi was surrounded. The door was yanked opened and the man was pulled outside.

Nick was in a whirlwind and being pushed out of the way. He tried to slide a film plate into his camera, but elbows and shoulders stopped him.

"You dirty scab!" people yelled. "Make him pay!"

Bobbling his film plate, he watched the man get slugged, punch after punch, as different people took turns. Then the man was being stripped, but Nick couldn't capture the spectacle.

"Strip him naked!" the crowd shouted. "March him downtown and shame him!"

Furiously, Nick jabbed at the camera until the film plate clicked into the right spot. At that point, people were moving away from him, parading the nude man up the street.

Pushing his way ahead of the mob, he turned around, started walking backward and looked through the view finder.

Except for shoes and socks, the man was completely naked, sheepishly holding his hands in front of his pelvis as the pickets taunted him and steered him toward downtown.

Quickly pressing the shutter, Nick knew he captured another photograph worthy of front page news.

112

CASPER

CASPER WAS with the men from Department Two. It was midday and he was grateful for the cold, May morning and extra sleep. Each minute, the crowd was growing larger and people were spilling onto the roads at Chestnut and Michigan.

He was standing on a packed sidewalk. The sidewalk where two men died yesterday. Dried blood had stained a section of the concrete. A section no one was standing on.

"Gonna be another busy day," Charlie said.

Casper looked at the crowd. People were dressed warmer than yesterday and conversing with one another in lighthearted, tense and somber dialogue, all at the same time. Most of them, Casper didn't recognize, but a feeling of comradery was unmistakable.

"Here they come," Hank said.

The troops were marching up Chestnut Hill, more soldiers than yesterday, and Casper sensed something different, as if he could feel their stares. Keeping his eyes on them, he listened as Tom Ramsey, business agent for the union, began addressing the crowd. He told them about telegrams that were sent to both President Roosevelt and the

Ohio Governor. And how the strongly worded cables requested the immediate removal of the troops. He said they demanded that Auto-Lite, Bingham, and Logan stay shut down, until negotiations are completed.

Every sentence Ramsey said was met with applause until a soldier threw a brick, hitting him in the ankle.

All at once, another brick storm ensued.

113

NICK

NICK WAS READY. He had been running from one intersection to another and had just captured an intense brick battle when a surging group of sympathizers pushed him onto a front porch. The quick action caused him to lose his footing and made him hug his camera as he braced for the fall. Instead, he felt two hands on his back, catching him and propping him upright.

"You okay?"

"Yeah," Nick responded. "Thanks."

The man introduced himself as the home owner.

"I work for the Cleveland newspaper," Nick replied.

An intense conversation followed. The man told him he had been fired from Auto-Lite a year ago for using the bathroom and wanted *those bastards* to pay. He told Nick to get as many photos as he could and show the world who Miniger and Minch really were.

Nick glanced at the pickets, then turned to the man and said, "How's about getting me up there? Should be a pretty good view."

He was pointing upward, motioning to the second floor

of the house. And, before he knew it, he was following the man inside.

Entering a cozy living room, the man led him upstairs and into a front bedroom.

"Want the window open?" the man asked.

He didn't have to answer. The man was already opening it and welcoming any shots Nick could get.

Leaning onto the window ledge, he poked his head outside and scanned the area. It was the perfect location, a house on the corner of Chestnut and Michigan. The unexpected vantage point led to an extraordinary photograph that documented the soldiers trying to reestablish their military line.

Changing his film plate, he kept his eyes on the evolving scene when the pickets began another brick attack. A moment later, sickening gas exploded, which quickly drifted into the room and ended his lucky viewpoint.

114

SAMMY

SAMMY PEEKED out from behind a house. "They're marchin' up the street," he said.

He and Carl arrived at the riot area after lunch and found an unmanned stone pile in someone's backyard. Since no one was using it, they set up a plan to hit as many soldiers as they could.

"They're almost in front," Sammy added.

He watched Carl bounce a stone in his hand, run through the side yard, throw the missile, and run back.

"Got a photographer," Carl snickered. "Beaned him in back."

Sammy laughed too. "Lemme see who I can hit," he said.

Stone in hand, he snuck alongside the house and paused at the front porch. The soldiers had stopped and were standing and waiting right in front of the house. The action was a block away and Sammy thought they must've been the backup troops that arrived last night.

Slowly, he squatted down and crept up to a shrub. He was a few yards from the soldiers and scanned their faces. Maybe he would recognize one of them; after all, they were probably his age, but he didn't know what part of Ohio they were from.

Setting his sights on the closest soldier, he thought about where to aim to maximize the most pain. Their thick uniforms and steel helmets protected most of their bodies, but their faces and hands were exposed. Springing from his hideout, he quickly hurled the stone then darted back to Carl.

"Got one," he said. "Popped him right in the ear."

They had a good laugh, imagining how it must've felt to be hit by a jagged stone, directly in the ear.

"I'm gonna get a Sergeant next—"

Sammy's words were stopped by a sharp jab in his lower back.

"Reach for the ceiling," a man's voice said. "Now!"

He raised his arms and cautiously glanced over his shoulder. Standing right behind him and Carl were two soldiers with their bayonets pointed.

"You're coming with us," one of the soldiers said.

Sammy was poked again. This time, it hurt.

"Where you takin' us?" Carl asked.

"To the factory. Now let's go."

They were told to drop what was in their hands and move to the driveway. As soon as Sammy approached the side yard, he took off running.

Leaping over a fence, he pushed a picket out of his way and sprinted down the road. Impressed by his own speed, he thought about his high school track team because he easily outran the soldier and Carl.

115

ORVILLE

Orville's platoon was ordered to hold the corner of Chestnut and Michigan Streets. It wasn't easy. The mob had an infinite supply of bricks and other missiles and he was getting pelted again. Earlier, he learned about a truck that delivered bricks and stones to the rioters and his unit was told to expect another long day of fighting.

The new offensive was underway and he was ordered to return as many bricks as he could. He tried to throw the way his dad taught him, but as he expected, his aim wasn't accurate. One time, his brick bounced off a telephone pole and hit another soldier. Nevertheless, the counter-offense worked. The volley drove back the crowd, giving Orville's bruises a reprieve, at least for a few minutes.

"Murderers!" someone shouted.

The bricks were coming back, flying in from every angle, except behind him.

He stepped backward.

"Hold your ground!" his Sergeant yelled.

His shoulder was hit, thrusting his body to the side and almost knocking him off balance.

"Hold your ground!" his Sergeant repeated.

The mob was getting closer to the soldiers. Bricks were flying faster and within seconds, his platoon was backpedaling down Chestnut Hill.

Out of the corner of his eye, he saw a fellow soldier get hit in the helmet. The force whipped the guy's head back and, in return, the soldier lifted his rifle and fired a shot. The bullet whistled over the rioters' heads, stopping the brick bombardment and halting their advancement.

Orders were shouted and he was marching up Chestnut Hill again.

116

NICK

NICK DODGED A STONE. A minute ago, he saw another photographer try to duck out of the way of an incoming brick. It didn't connect with the man's body, but struck his camera. Nick didn't want a member of *his* club to get hit, but it also eliminated his competition.

Checking his camera, he blew a puff of air at the lens, tested its focus, then held it to his eyes.

A heated exchange of bricks was clouding the sky. The pickets were yelling things like *baby killers* and *murderers* and now, the soldiers were trying to push the pickets back into submission.

A siren blasted.

Tear gas canisters were fired and, within minutes, gas had obscured his sight.

Retreating down the street, he coughed vapors from his lungs, zoomed in on the scene and pressed the shutter.

117

SAMMY

SAMMY WONDERED where they took Carl. He was on his own now, wandering down Crane Lane and heading away from the action. The back alley offered a hidden view and he enjoyed seeing into people's private lives. Eyeing a clothes line, he analyzed the clean laundry, laughing at the underwear and slips. Another yard had a few toys scattered around, a ball, a kite tethered to a doorknob and a bicycle.

He stopped walking, reached into his pocket and pulled out a stick of beef jerky. He had found the dried meat hanging in someone's shed and stuffed as many pieces as he could into his pockets. It was salty and satisfied his hunger.

Biting off another piece, he chewed the leathery food and eyed the bike. It would've been quite the find if it had tires and a seat.

He started walking again. This time, he decided to go back to the riot zone and see if he could find Carl.

118

CASPER

Tear gas and bricks dispersed the men of Department Two away from Chestnut Hill. The crowd was forced deeper into the neighborhood by a blanket of gas clouds.

"Let's cut this way and head over to Koolmotor," Hank said.

Casper wasn't about to let the young guardsmen win this round and followed his buddy down the street. The service station was a picket stronghold and they were only a block away. He appreciated the sympathizers and spectators and wanted their support, but moving from one area to another was getting more difficult.

Weaving their way through the masses, they turned onto Elm Street. Casper looked at the houses. The once peaceful road had taken a beating with a slew of broken windows and ravaged front yards, but each porch was filled with home owners and spectators, all encouraging the pickets.

They were half way down the street when a commotion began and voices were raised. Then a soldier appeared in the crowd, with a drawn pistol. People were shouting at him as he forged a path and marched straight toward a crowded porch.

Casper eyed the men and women standing in the small space as the soldier boldly walked up to them and shouted, "Who threw that brick?"

"Baby killer!" one of the women responded.

"That brick!" he said. "It came from over here. Now, who threw it?"

The soldier pointed his gun from one person to another and yelled, "Who threw it?"

No one answered.

Casper closely watched as the soldier moved in on one of the men.

"Was it you?" he asked. "Huh?"

The man laughed.

Holding his breath, Casper waited for an inevitable clash as the soldier raised his gun, then whacked the man on the side of his head. The gun went off, sending a bullet into the ceiling and causing one of the women to faint.

"They've killed a woman!" someone shouted.

Confusion blanketed the crowd and, as Casper scanned the restless group, he spotted soldiers among them.

It didn't take long for the pickets to explode and chaos to follow.

Within seconds, incoming gas bombs dropped into the crowd, clearing everyone from the street.

119

NICK

Nick was watching through his view finder, looking for his next shot, when he noticed a young boy approaching the area of Champlain and Michigan Streets. A fierce brick volley was underway, separating soldiers and pickets, and the youngster was way too close. Nick zoomed in looking for a parent. Or any adult. But the boy was alone.

He couldn't have been older than nine or ten and Nick's pulse raced at seeing the ominous site. Then he spotted a newspaper bag slung over the boy's shoulder.

With his breath held, Nick watched the situation unfold.

The boy was digging into his pocket and pulled out a handkerchief. Then holding it high in the air, he walked to the battle area.

Nick swallowed hard, watching his every move.

With the white cloth waving, the newsboy stepped into the line of fire and, suddenly, the brick throwing stopped. As he moved through the riot zone, he skillfully threw newspaper after newspaper from house to house and, as he walked down the street, the brick throwing in front of him stopped and immediately picked up behind him.

Awestruck by the phenomenon, Nick forgot to press the

shutter and wanted to talk to the boy. Darting through a hail of bricks that didn't stop for him, he yelled, "Stop! Newsboy! Stop!"

The boy was leaving the riot zone, tossing newspapers as he moved and placing his handkerchief back into his pocket.

Rushing to his side, Nick grabbed his arm and said, "You did it! You accomplished what the National Guard and mediators could *not* do!"

The boy looked surprised. And worried. And determined.

"I couldn't let my paper route go and have my customer quit," he said.

Nick listened as the boy explained how his father was sick and his paper route was his family's only source of income. He truly was an extraordinary boy, full of boldness and gumption.

"Weren't you scared?" he asked.

"A little," the boy replied. "But I prayed."

Nick couldn't take his eyes off the young lad. A boy doing what men could not do.

"*I* didn't do anything to the soldiers," the boy added. "So, I thought they would let me by. I was kinda scared when I got to Chestnut and Michigan, because that's where they shot the fellas."

Nick stood in awe as the boy left. Then he yelled, "Wait! I need a picture!"

The boy turned around and smiled at him.

It was the best picture Nick took.

120

ORVILLE

ORVILLE WAS grateful to be inside the factory. He didn't care that it was late afternoon or that the cot he was sitting on was hard as a board. The only thing he wanted to do was sleep. His boots were already off and he was unwrapping his spiral shin puttees. As the leg bindings went lax, his pants ballooned to their natural form. Earlier, a flying piece of glass struck him in the lower leg and he wanted to make sure the material protected him from a wound.

He had aches all over his body. Not only from being a target all day, but from trying to throw as many bricks as the other soldiers.

Rolling up his pant legs, he eyed his naked shins. No wounds were visible, just corkscrew imprints and blueish bruises. He fared better than a lot of other soldiers who had bloody, torn uniforms.

Rubbing the indented skin, he glanced around the room. A reserved row of military cots lined the wall and were filled with men injured from bricks and glass and sickened from fumes. They were told not to tell anyone how many soldiers were wounded. As if he had time to talk.

Removing the rest of his uniform, he pulled a blanket over his body and fell asleep.

121

CASPER

SUPPERTIME PROVED to have a lulling effect on the activities and the crowd became smaller. Casper and the men of Department Two took the opportunity to go home and eat. Tear gas and brick throwing drained his energy and he didn't want to go back, but Charlie told him they needed to keep the pressure on because a resolution was near.

He couldn't remember what his wife cooked and his nap wasn't long enough. Forty minutes later, she woke him up.

Accompanying him to the strike zone, he told her she needed to leave by sunset and left her with the other wives. Then he and Hank approached the military line. Knowing the respite gave the soldiers an opportunity to expand their occupation, they hunted out the extended border. It had been pushed further into the neighborhood, significantly, and now was at the intersections of Elm and Ontario and Michigan and Lagrange.

Word had circulated earlier and bottles were added to the pickets' arsenal.

Casper brought pop bottles and Hank brought a one gallon jug. Others joined in and contributed their share.

Soon enough, it was crowded again and everyone was ready for the night.

122

ORVILLE

SLEEPING WAS NOT EASY. The fellow in the cot next to Orville was groaning from a welt on his face and every time he turned over Orville woke up.

Sunset was hours away and daylight in the room made it difficult to doze off.

Finding his spiral puttee, he unrolled the material and draped it over his eyes. The light was doused, but his mind was active. He couldn't stop thinking about the bricks and how he stepped backward when the other soldiers didn't. And how they all bragged about drawing blood with their bayonets. Yet his was clean.

His dad told him the military would make him a man. But he didn't feel courageous. He felt like a coward.

Sighing, he rolled to his side and wished it was all over.

123

SAMMY

"WHERE'VE YA BEEN?" Sammy asked.

He ran into Carl on Mulberry Street, hours after the soldiers captured him. At first, he wasn't sure it was him because whoever it was seemed to be slinking away from the crowd. But he caught up with the guy and confirmed it was his friend.

Carl looked stunned and bruised and bloody.

Sammy repeated his question.

"They took me to their headquarters," Carl replied, "inside the factory."

"Did they shake ya up or somethin'?"

"Yeah, they punched me a lot. But I spit in their faces."

Carl didn't look right and he wasn't looking at Sammy.

"Looks like you're gettin' a shiner," Sammy said. "And ya got dried blood on your ear. Both of 'em."

He watched as his buddy put his fingers over his black eye, gently patting the bruised area.

"Did they scare ya?" Sammy asked.

"Nah," Carl replied. "I ain't scared. Told 'em that too."

Sammy eyed his buddy. He seemed nervous or dazed,

looking over his shoulder and back at the crowd. Then his friend simply walked away.

"You're not goin' home, are ya?" Sammy yelled.

"I'm hungry," Carl replied.

"Are ya comin' back?"

"Don't know. But if I do, I'm bringin' my BB gun."

124

NICK

Nick asked a picket where he could get some grub.

"Buckeye Brewing," the man replied. "Good food. An' sometimes it's free."

"Where is it?" Nick asked.

"Corner of Bush and Michigan. It's part of the beer plant."

Suppertime had already passed and Nick hoped there would be food left for him. Reaching into his pocket, he pulled out a piece of paper, torn from a larger map, and studied the grid work streets of the riot zone. The intersection was east and only three blocks away.

He began his trek, walking the opposite direction of most people. Mulberry Street was the first crossroad and, looking south, he spotted a line of parked cars as far as he could see. They probably filled every block, both sides, up to the Maumee River. It seemed the dwindling daylight wasn't going to stop the sympathizing and, from the looks of the individuals, the soldiers were in for a long night.

Another block passed.

Stepping over railroad tracks, he was about to cross Bush Street when he spotted a funny billboard reflecting a setting sun. It was a cartoon character of a little man holding a beer tray and winking at him. He winked back, wishing he had just one more blank film plate to document Toledo's peculiar sense of humor.

The corner bar was near.

Opening the door, he entered the establishment. It was active and jovial, as if people had money and the economy wasn't miserable. Beer was flowing and music was playing and there was food on a side table.

He stood at the back of the line, counting the people in front of him and eyeing the stack of hotdogs.

"Did ya get some good shots?"

Someone was talking to him. He didn't feel like responding, but he turned around anyway. It was an older man, wiping his hands on an apron, and looking directly into his eyes.

"Aren't you a photographer?" the man asked.

"Yeah, yeah," Nick replied. "And I got some good shots. Really good shots."

"That's good," the man said. "Who ya work for?"

"Cleveland newspaper."

He felt the eyes of the old man looking him over.

"Do you fellas share your pictures?" he asked. "You know, with other papers. Like Toledo's."

"Yeah, we do," Nick replied. "They decide whose pictures are the best. And those are the ones they print."

The man nodded, then stared at his face and asked, "Whose side you on?"

Nick looked at the old man, then glanced at the hotdogs and said, "The strikers. Of course."

"I see," the man replied. "What was the best picture you took?"

The man wasn't going to let the conversation go. Nick thought about his answer and what the man wanted to hear. They were all astounding photographs and newsworthy.

Action shots of the soldiers, action shots of the pickets and the death of a young man.

"They're all good pictures," he replied.

"I see," the man said. "But really. Pick one."

"The newsboy," Nick said without thinking. "Yeah. The newsboy."

The man didn't respond, but continued to stare. After a few awkward moments, he finally spoke and said, "Come over to this table and have a seat. I'll fix ya a plate."

An hour had passed. He chatted with the old man the entire time, talking about everything from the strike to the economy and the Great War. Drinking the last of his beer, he thanked the old man for the free meal, then got up and left. When he stepped outside, nighttime had arrived and he made his way out of the area.

125

CASPER

A NIGHT PLAN was put into place. Casper and Hank were placing wheelbarrows near the service station and Lester and Bill were making homemade smoke bombs, by adding chemicals to glass bottles. The goal was to push the troops back, one block east, from the intersection of Champlain and Elm to the front of the office building. Smoke bombs wouldn't be expected and there was never a shortage of bricks. Casper wanted the diversion to work and deliver maximum damage.

Everything was set. Street lighting had long been extinguished and Lester and Bill had secretly made their way on top of a roof. Brick snipers were in place and Casper was eyeing the moonlit helmets of the troops. They were idly standing in the intersection, talking amongst themselves and oblivious to the plan.

He glanced at Hank and said, "Hoof, you ready?"

His buddy nodded.

Taking a deep breath, Casper eyed the troops once more, then let out a shrieking whistle. Smoke bombs were launched and bricks were thrown. They were making progress and pushing the soldiers backward until a car, headlights beaming, drove into the area and broke the momentum.

"Where the hell do these people think they're goin'?" Hank said.

Suddenly, wheelbarrows and brick snipers were exposed and tear gas canisters were fired.

Fleeing billowing gas, Casper and the other pickets chased the car, throwing bricks as they ran until the driver sped out of the area.

He was a block away from the troops and realized reassembling their plan was impossible. The troops had advanced and a bombing of tear gas was being released.

126

SAMMY

SAMMY LISTENED to the rattling of Carl's BB gun. His buddy was shaking the weapon, guessing at the remaining amount of ammunition. He didn't bring a fully loaded gun because he didn't have any money.

A few minutes ago, they had a good laugh when Carl hit a paddy wagon, causing a nearby soldier to dive for cover.

Sammy watched his buddy lift the gun to his shoulder, aim, and fire another shot.

"Damn it!" Carl said. "The guy moved."

"Any BBs left?" Sammy asked.

Carl shook the gun.

"Only a few," his buddy said.

"Let's get outta here," Sammy said. "I'm bored."

127

ORVILLE

ORVILLE WASN'T RESTED, but he was on night duty, partnered with another soldier and assigned to find snipers. They were told BB guns were being used, fired at the troops from different angles and it was his job to find as many snipers as he could.

The area had quieted down and the crowd was dwindling.

Orville and his partner set their sights on a particularly crafty sniper who was shooting from a somewhere along Dove Lane. The capture of this sharpshooter would assure Orville a successful story to tell his dad and he was ready to skewer someone, if it came to that.

Avoiding bright patches of moonlight, they were quietly moving down the alleyway when Orville spotted a tree-house. Ready to seize a victory, he motioned to his partner, silently climbed up the ladder, and peeked inside. The little room was empty.

More shots were fired. This time, they were coming from Elm and Champlain.

Hustling to the street, he scanned the remaining pickets. They were clumped into groups, smoking and talking.

"It came from over there," his partner said.

Orville pointed his bayonet, weaved his way around the pickets and reached the back of Koolmotor. Two men were in the yard, acting nonchalant, and having a discussion. He analyzed their movements, wondering which one was the sniper. One of the men was of normal stature, puffing on a half-smoked cigar. The other was a big guy, much bigger than Orville, and an unlikely sniper. But it's always someone you least expect.

"That's him," Orville said.

Stomping through the yard, Orville walked right up to the big man, poked him in the back and said, "March! We're taking you in!"

The bear like man looked over his shoulder and said, "What'd I do?"

"You know what you did," Orville spat. "Where's your BB gun?"

"I don't have a gun," the man replied. "I'm a newspaper man."

"Sure you are," Orville replied. "And I'm a photographer. Now move it!"

He poked the man's lower back, making sure they guy felt it.

"I'm a newspaper ma—"

"Save your speech," his partner replied. "You can tell it to the Captain."

Orville, with the help of the other soldier, moved the man from the yard and onto Elm Street. Every few steps, he poked at the lumbering bear, making him jump. And, whenever he slowed down, he poked him harder.

The man's claim was unbelievable and Orville knew it was impossible. The guy looked sloppy with dripping sweat, a soaked shirt, and hair plastered to his brow.

"Could you let me slow down a little?" the man said. "I've got bum arches."

Orville eyed his feet. The man did look like he was in pain, but nonetheless, he gave him a poke and said, "Keep moving."

They made it to the factory and Orville's group went inside.

Parading his captured sniper, he walked the big man to the makeshift headquarters, a room inside the plant, where a guard began to pat him down.

"I'm a newspaper man," the guy repeated.

"You're no newspaper man," the guard said. "You're a Communist. We've had our eyes on you for some time."

Orville watched the spectacle of a skinny guardsman patting down a fat man, retrieving a flask and room key from the guy's pockets.

"I see you're one of those rich Communists," the guard said. "Staying at the Commodore Perry Hotel. You outta be ashamed of yourself."

Orville listened as the man tried to convince them he was who he said he was. The guard scoffed and told Orville to remain with his prisoner, until the captain conducted an interrogation. The man clumsily leaned against a stack of metal plates and started to reach into his shirt pocket.

"Careful!" Orville said and pointed his bayonet at his face.

A handkerchief was pulled out and the man showed it to Orville, then wiped his brow.

Moments later, the captain walked up to the man.

"Who are you?" the Captain asked.

"I'm a newspaper man," he replied.

"Where's your credentials?"

"I haven't any. But I'm a newspaper man. From New York."

Orville watched the big man sweat, like a sniper would, when he got caught.

"Oh, no you're not," the Captain said. "You're a Communist. You've been pointed out to us."

"I'm staying at the Commodore Perry Hotel," the man said. "See the key?"

"I see, they take pretty good care of you New York Communists. Putting you up in that fancy hotel when our local boys have to sleep on park benches."

Orville listened as the conversation escalated. The captain quizzed the man about what train he arrived on. Then a discussion about standard and daylight savings time stalled any progress of identification and caused the captain to repeatedly asked the same question.

"Lemme see your hands," the Captain said. "Brick dust will tell us if you're a labor agitator."

The big man held out his hands, palms up, then palms down.

"How did you get through the military line?" the Captain asked.

"I walked thru," came the reply.

Orville shook his head at his answer. The captain continued to interrogate until he was interrupted by a legitimate, local, newspaper man.

"His name is Heywood Broun," the newsman said. "A renowned columnist from New York City."

128

CASPER

IT WAS close to midnight and people were leaving the area. Casper and the men of Department Two had gathered on Lester's front porch.

"Ramsey told me they're close to a resolution," Charlie said. "Any day now, we'll be goin' back to work."

Casper thought of the battered factory. Almost every window was broken, the permanent first floor window grates were mutilated and bricks and debris littered Champlain Street. Then he thought about the fireballs he threw inside and wondered what damage they caused.

"I wonder how the press machines faired," Hank said.

"We're gonna find out," Charlie replied. "Soon enough."

PART XI

There is no greater calling than to serve your fellow men.
There is no greater contribution than to help the weak.
There is no greater satisfaction than to have done it well.
~ Walter Reuther

129

EDITH

EDITH WAS in a conference room at the Commodore Perry Hotel. It was a makeshift office she shared with Genevieve and Doris, on the fourth floor. The room wasn't big, but she had a view of the pretty brick building across the street. Mr. Moore arranged for a table, three chairs and three telephones to be set up, along with three typewriters. At the moment, their job was to call the employees, those who did not strike, tell them they would receive one week's pay and be notified when it was safe to return.

Earlier, when she walked into the lobby, she saw Tom Ramsey, other union chiefs and Washington mediators getting into an elevator. They were scheduled to meet with Mr. Minch because a resolution was reached and the final touches were needed.

Concentrating on her first call, she stumbled through the conversation and when asked if the strike was officially over she said, "I think so. They're working through everything right now."

Then the worker asked how secure his job was, wondering if the strikers were going to get first dibs.

She didn't know the answer to that one either and said

as much.

"I really need that job," he replied. "Can you tell them that for me?"

"Yes," she said. But she didn't think it would make a difference.

Hanging up, she was about to dial the next number when she heard Mr. Moore calling her name.

"Edith," he said. "Can you have these notes typed up within the hour?"

He handed her several pages of scribbled words.

"Yes," she said. "What kind of format do you want?"

"Just bullet points," he replied. "We want to see the details outlined."

"How's everything going?" Genevieve asked.

"Pretty good," he replied. "Mr. Minch isn't happy, but is he ever?"

Edith laughed a surprisingly loud laugh. Mr. Moore was a good man and funny too. As he hobbled to the door, he turned around and said, "Edith, you're doing a good job. All you girls are doing a good job."

She didn't know what to say. She'd never been thanked so sincerely before. Then she thought of something and replied, "So are you, Mr. Moore."

He smiled and hobbled away.

"What do the notes say?" Genevieve asked.

"Yeah, let's see 'em," Doris added.

Spreading them onto the table, she, Genevieve and Doris eyed the messy handwriting.

"This one says the plant will remain closed until negotiations are finalized," Edith said, "And Auto-Lite *must*, and Mr. Moore underlined that word *must*, recognize the union and agree to negotiate with them."

"That's good," Genevieve replied. "Look at this one, it says all employees who walked out to strike can return to their jobs. Immediately."

Edith thought of the man on the phone and his desperate voice and what that meant for him.

"This one says they're gonna get a five percent pay increase," Doris said. "I wonder if that applies to us too."

More money would be nice, but more importantly, Edith was grateful the rioting was over, and so was her grandmother.

"Looks like the strikers did it," Genevieve said. "They got what they wanted."

"If they didn't," Doris replied, "all of Toledo was ready to strike. A *general* strike, where *every* worker, in *every* kind of work, would walk out. Wouldn't that be something?"

Edith thought of a conversation she had with her grandmother. She told Edith back in the old country people couldn't strike like this because they would've been punished or killed.

"I read up to twenty thousand people were in the strike zone," Edith said. "And we made the front page of every single newspaper in the country."

"Oh my," Doris replied. "We're famous."

"I heard this was the largest military display in peace time," Genevieve said. "Ever. In the history of Ohio."

Edith looked at the notes, wondering where to start when Doris became very quiet, then said, "Oh dear. Look at this one."

She was pointing to a page where Mr. Moore's handwriting was a beautiful, swirling cursive.

"What does it say?" Edith asked.

Doris didn't reply. Her eyes looked misty as she bowed her head and walked to the window.

Edith and Genevieve looked at the paper.

Written, over and over, were the words *Frank Hubay* and *Steve Cyigon*. The two men killed.

Releasing a deep, long sigh, Edith collected the papers, took her seat and began to type the details of the resolution.

130

NICK

Nick arrived back in Cleveland. It felt good to be in the newsroom where the hustle and bustle didn't include bricks and gas. His body ached, not from being hit - no brick touched him - but from rushing around, morning till night, angling for a shot.

Leaning against a desk, he listened as the editor addressed the newsroom staff. The man led his speech with congratulations to Nick and his *runner*, the man who transported the film plates, each night, back to Cleveland. He said the pictures were better than any other photographer's, simply extraordinary, like the event itself. Then shot glasses and whiskey were passed around and a toast was made.

Downing the booze, Nick thought about the pickets and the guardsmen and the newsboy and the resolution. It was an extraordinary event. Remarkable in every way. He wanted to marvel in his thoughts, but they were interrupted by the editor.

"Folks," the man said, "we've got a deadline to meet. Get back to work."

131

SAMMY

SAMMY WAS LISTENING to a new friend, an old guy, recount a story about how he ran moonshine to a downtown building.

"Back in the day," the old guy said, "They paid me to drive a car to Jefferson and Ontario, downtown"

"In Toledo?" Sammy asked.

"Yeah, here," he replied. "There was a secret door, a big one, the size of a truck, and it would open. And, I'd drive in."

Sammy tried to imagine a big door hidden in a downtown brick building.

"Inside was an elevator, big enough for the car," the old guy continued. "so I drove in and it took me to the third floor. And that's where they unloaded the loot."

An elevator big enough for a car didn't seem likely, but Sammy wanted to remain on good terms and accepted the lies.

"I got a story too," Sammy said. "I was at Auto-Lite."

"During the strike?" the old guy asked. "Did ya work in the factory?"

"Nah," he replied. "I was what they called a *sympathizer*."

"I would've gone," the old guy responded, "but I was *indisposed.*"

Sammy didn't know what that meant, but got the old guy's gist.

"What'd ya do as a *sympathizer*?"

"Used a BB gun," he replied, "I shot up things. Even got a couple of the soldiers."

Sammy thought of Carl's BB gun and how he didn't get to use it, but if he did he was sure he would've hit everything he targeted.

"They were strikin' for a safer factory, right?" the old guy asked.

"I dunno. Maybe."

"Did they win?"

"Don't know that either," Sammy replied.

He didn't care who won or lost. It wasn't going to affect him either way. Studying a jigsaw puzzle on a table, he picked up an end piece and was about to fit it in when he heard his name being called.

"Samuel Nichols?"

"Yeah?" he replied.

"Come with me," a guard said. "The judge is ready to hear your plea."

132

VERN

VERN SAT on his back patio, drinking whiskey and talking with his brother. They were having a polite conversation about the Detroit Tigers. But Vern didn't care about Mickey Cochrane or how he was named the Tiger's new player-manager. Nevertheless, he continued with the superficial dialogue.

Taking a sip of his drink, he halfheartedly listened while he thought about his time at Auto-Lite. His last day there had been the *all-nighter* and, after the strike ended, he wasn't offered a job. None of the new hires were and tomorrow, he would be looking for work. Again.

Coming back to the present moment, he glanced at his wife. She was sitting next to his sister-in-law, rubbing her fingers on a glass of iced tea. Neither woman was talking or even looking at one another. Vern thought of the many heated conversations all four of them had over the strike. One night, his wife became so fiery in defending him, she lost her voice. He never thought peace would come, but there they were, all four of them, sitting on his back patio.

"How's about a game of pinochle?" he asked.

His wife shot a look at him, the one that means he shouldn't have opened his mouth. After a few awkward moments, she looked at his sister-in-law and said, "Okay. I'll get the cards."

133

ORVILLE

Orville's kid brother punched him in the leg.

"Ow!" Orville said. "Watch it. I still got bruises."

"Come on," his brother said. "What's wrong with you. Let's play."

The moment Orville got home, things seemed different.

He was thankful to be away from the pickets and the gas and his Sergeant, but things seemed different. His dad joked with him and said his two weeks in Toledo was the National Guard's version of the Great War. Orville didn't know what fighting on foreign soil was like and didn't think his dad's joke was funny. Normally, he would've laughed. Most of the things his dad said *were* funny. But things seemed different and his laugh was a fake smile.

His model cars, a swell collection, no longer excited him. And he didn't care about his bicycle or his brother wanting to ride it. He couldn't put his finger on it, but things seemed different.

"How about a game of jacks?" his brother asked. "Or we can play with my soldiers. What do ya think about that?"

Orville heard his brother's questions, but instead of answering, he looked at his hands. They were his own hands, he knew that much, but they looked different. Aged by cracked nails, scratches and cuts.

"What's that matter?" his brother asked. "Worry about scratching Pauline at the dance?"

He had nearly forgotten about his graduation. It didn't seem important anymore. Even Pauline noticed things were different. He couldn't explain it to her, but was happy she took him seriously.

Pondering his future, he began to think about a military summer camp when his brother interrupted his thoughts.

"Here," his brother said. "Catch!"

A ball came flying at Orville's face. His heart jumped as he ducked from the incoming missile.

"What's wrong with you?" his brother asked.

Orville didn't know. Things were different and he no longer wanted to play. But he did it anyway.

134

CASPER

Charlie's basement was filled with the men of Department Two. Joe, Lester, Bill, Hank the Hoof, and the rest of the men were sitting around, smiling and laughing and talking about their return to Auto-Lite. The strike caused a lot of damage and the first few days back were spent repairing the punch press machines *and* adding safety guards. But the foremen hadn't changed. The punch press operators still had to wait their turn to work, but now when they sat on the bench they were being paid for their time. And their wages were better. And the Sixty B's were fairer.

Although Department Two was calm, Casper heard it was a different experience working on the production line. That department was large and had some workers who chose not to strike, until the forced shutdown. When the plant reopened, tensions between strikers and strikebreakers had not subsided. People said it was hostile and contentious and name calling was common. He was glad his group was in unison and knew if he had to work alongside a strike-breaker a punch or two would've been thrown.

Sitting back in his chair, he brought a cigarette to his lips and took a satisfying drag. 1934 was only half over and the first six month had been quite a gamble. The earlier strike in February lasted only five days because Auto-Lite falsely agreed to recognize the local union. *This* strike lasted two months, April to June, and because of the mediators and the government's presence they would have a lasting resolution. He didn't receive a drop of income during either strike and couldn't have done it without his wife's ingenuity and support. It had been burdensome and painful and exuberant and euphoric. But most importantly, it had been victorious. Local 18384 had been recognized and that meant acknowledgement of seniority, livable wages and worker protection.

"You'll be happy to know," Charlie said. "We won the best bargaining point of them all."

"Which one was that?" Lester asked.

"Minch," Charlie replied. "The point we won was Minch can no longer be at the plant. *And* he has to move out of Toledo."

Casper let out a big howl and clapped his hands. Life was great and everyone in Department Two was happy. Slapping Hank on the back, he asked, "How's about another snort?"

It was a rhetorical question. Gin was already flowing.

NOTEWORTHY

Deaths: On May 24, 1934, Steve Cyigon (20) and Frank Hubay (27) were, like most Toledoans, curious bystanders at the strike. During the heat of the battle, rifle fire erupted and they were both shot and killed.

On May 28, 1934, at St. Stephens Church in Toledo, a joint funeral was held honoring the two men. They are both buried in Calvary Cemetery.

Types of wounds reported: Rifle shots in groin, legs, arms, abdomen, heel, shoulder, and wrist. Bayonet wounds to the back and thighs. Loss of an eye from a gas shell hit. Injuries and unconsciousness from being hit with bricks. Illness and headaches from tear gas and sickening gas. Broken bones from being trampled. Various slingshot injuries.

Gas used: Tear gas, chloracetophenone, the most common. DM gas, diphenolaminechlorasine. KOCN gas, which is a combination gas.

Incidents reported in the *Vistula District* neighborhood (not all inclusive): Due to gas permeating into neighborhood homes, residents circulated a petition asking for the troops to be removed. After receiving 150 signatures, they sent it to the Ohio Governor.

An Auto-Lite employee was at his home on Champlain Street. As he sat in his living room, tear gas began to pour in. Then he was shot in the leg.

A stick of dynamite was found on the premises of a home on Champlain Street. People residing there were held on suspicious person charges until one of the accused said he was employed by his father, a contractor, and the dynamite was used in the business.

Sitting in his front living room, a resident was grazed by a *streak of light* that whizzed by him. Realizing it was a gas bomb, he tried to get out of his house but was trapped by the crowd, pressed against his door. He was sealed in the room with the fumes.

Courtroom drama: There are several renditions of the courtroom trial. The one depicted in chapter 26 is the version recounted by Charles Rigby's oral history documented in *I Remember Like Today: The Auto-Lite Strike of 1934* (Michigan State University Press, 1988) written by Philip A. Korth and Margaret R. Beegle.

However, the Toledo News-Bee noted the drama in a slightly different way. Forty-six strikers and sympathizers were being held in the city's jail. The judge, Judge Stuart, ordered deputies to bring him only the leaders from the group. He wanted the preliminary hearing for the leaders to decide the fate of all 46. Ted Selander, Norman Meyers, Sam Pollock, Charles Rigby, and James Roland were summoned. However, before these men could be brought to court, the courthouse's corridors were jammed with pickets and sympathizers demanding to see Judge Stuart. When he emerged from his chamber, he was met by a group of women strikers who hounded him for the release of the all 46 men. He refused. Then the five men arrived in court. The unruly crowd could not be controlled and the judge threatened to arrest anyone making a disturbance. Continually heckled and booed, Judge Stuart eventually released the men, not before giving them a lecture.

Mistaken identity: According to the Toledo News-Bee, the covered walkway, connecting the office building to the factory, was the home for a family of sparrows. Whenever the birds flew out of their nests, they looked like flying tear gas canisters and caused the pickets to duck.

Newsman for the Detroit Times: During the strike, the Toledo News-Bee wrote an article about a Detroit reporter who arrived in the riot zone on a cold, rainy night. Wearing only a light-weight suit, he said he "couldn't take it" anymore and knocked on a door in the strike area. Asking to borrow a coat, he received one, but due to the commotion of the night, he forgot to get the address and even forgot the street. The article announced that he was looking for the kind man who loaned him the coat and wanted to give it back.

O. E. Fuller: The Toledo News-Bee wrote an article about O. E. Fuller, the newsboy who single-handedly stopped the battle, if only for a moment, to deliver newspapers. The boy was noted as saying he needed to maintain his route to financially support his sick father and family. Chapter 119 tells the story.

The events in this book take place in 1934 and in the

1930 census, the boy was listed with his mother and father, brother and sister living on Superior Street in Toledo. However, the 1940 census shows him living on Champlain Street. Notably absent in the household was his father's name.

Virgil Gladieux: Per the ToledoWalleye website, Virgil Gladieux owned Buddy Box Lunch Company located in the strike area in 1934. Sympathetic to the strikers, he gave away free coffee and donuts in the morning and hotdogs in the afternoon. When the strikebreakers were held overnight, Auto-Lite called him to see if he would deliver food. He turned them down. In the 1940 census, Virgil and his family lived in the strike area, on Magnolia Street.

Virgil would go on the become the owner of several Toledo sports teams: the Mercurys, Buckeyes, Blades, Hornets, and Golddiggers (1946-86).

Thomas Ramsey: Working at City Auto Stamping, Tom Ramsey was pivotal in organizing the United Auto Workers Local 18384. Later, he became a leader for the Auto Workers Federal Labor Union, founded in Detroit, MI, in 1935. He was considered a *progressive outsider* and had to prove to a doubtful population the value of joining a union.

National Guardsmen: On Saturday, June 2, 1934, the Ohio National Guardsmen were happy to be relieved of strike duty. The soldiers were paid $3 per day.

June 1934. Ohio National Guardsmen. Photo altered for 1934 newspaper printing

Heywood Broun: An American journalist, editor and sportswriter, Heywood Broun worked in New York City. He was known for good stories, drinking whiskey and his wonderful character. He wrote about his Auto-Lite ordeal in his column and after his interrogation about who he was and what he was doing there, he said "I'm not quite so friendly to the National Guard as I was when I wrote my column earlier in the day. I still think it's silly and aimless to throw at the soldiers, but if that provost marshal wants a good punch in the nose he has only to name his time and his alley."

Chapter 127 tells the story of his adventure in Toledo.

September 1933. Heywood Broun (right) pictured with Howard Davis.

Charles Rigby: A leader of the men of Department Two, Charlie Rigby worked tirelessly to organize the Auto-Lite workers to strike. When the strike ended, he was quoted as saying, "I finally got at their membership book (referring to Auto-Lite's so called *union*). I had a good soul hand it to me one day. They laid it down accidentally on purpose, you know."

In future years, he would go on to become an international representative for the United Auto Workers. He died in 1977 and is buried in Woodlawn Cemetery.

November 1945. Cleveland UAW Strike Leaders. Left to right: Charles Rigby, Paul E. Miley, Hardy Merrell.

September 1934. Caption on back of photo: "Charged with stealing the love of a watchman, Mrs. J. Arthur Minch (above), wife of the Vice President of the Electric Auto-Lite Co; at Toledo, O,. was the defendant in a $100,000 alienation of affections suit. The charges were made by "name redacted". She alleged her husband, who had been employed as a guard at the Minch home during the Auto-Lite Co. strike, had kept trysts with the industrialist's wife."

J. Arthur Minch: Known for *blowing his stack* and name calling, Mr. Minch was immediately transferred, following the settlement, to a plant in Port Huron, Michigan. It was said that after the strike, his picture hung in the factory and every time his name was mentioned, workers would throw coils and other auto parts at it.

Clement Miniger: An American industrialist, Mr. Miniger founded the Electric Auto-Lite Co in 1911. A self-made man, he made a quick fortune and Auto-Lite was successful until automobile manufacturers started producing the same parts for their vehicles in their own factories. However, at some point during the depression, the plant briefly made electric clocks.

After the strike, Auto-Lite merged with another company. He stepped down as the President and became Chairman of the Board until his death. At age 69, he died of heart disease in 1944.

Sheriff David Krieger: When David Krieger ran for office, he was supported by Clement Miniger. When the strike began, he approached fifty Toledo policemen, recently laid off, and asked them to join his forces. All fifty men declined.

The Toledo News-Bee ran an article about him saying that during intense rioting, at 5:15pm, the sheriff remembered dinner was waiting for him. Abruptly, he left Auto-Lite. Then returned an hour later when the rioting had quieted.

Sixty B's: Charles Bedaux, a millionaire, established the Bedaux System. To improve departmental efficiencies, manual work was measured through rating assessments and time studies, then converted into fractions of a minute called a Bedaux Unit or B. It is a point system where work, completed in a specific amount of time, equals a form of payment.

Aftermath: On June 5, 1934, the doors to Auto-Lite reopened and the workers returned to work. From most accounts, it took a while for the strikers and strikebreakers to forgive one another.

In 1962, Auto-Lite closed the Champlain Street location and moved its operations to other plants. Employees were offered the option to transfer, hundreds of miles away, or lose their small pensions. While some took the opportunity, most declined. When the plant officially closed, employees who worked for Auto-Lite for 30 years and under the age of 50 received no pension. However, the pension qualifying employees received \$20-\$50 per month.

Auto-Lite's buildings: After the plant closed in 1962, the four-story factory building stood emptied and abandoned until sometime around 1999 when it was torn down. Auto-Lite's office building, built in 1890, is still standing and used for other purposes.

June 1, 1934. Caption on back of photo: "Demonstrating the strength to back up threats of a general strike, organized labor paraded in Toledo, O. After the parade, union members and sympathizers gathered in Courthouse Square, where a crowd of over 15,000 heard speeches by labor leaders."

Memorial: Union Park Memorial is a small park located in the northeast corner of Champlain and Elm Streets. It is dedicated to the Auto-Lite strike and a plaque on the site reads:

"As the conflict escalated into civil war, Governor George White ordered Ohio's largest peacetime deployment of National Guard units. Machine guns were mounted near the Elm Street Bridge and other strategic points. Efforts to quell the rioting evolved into hand-to-hand combat, with strikers and guardsmen battling with bricks and tear gas in the streets of the North End. On May 24, 1934, during the "Battle of Chestnut Hill," guardsmen fired into the crowd, killing onlookers Steve Cyigon and Frank Hubay. Under pressure of a general strike, Auto-Lite's management agreed to recognize the union, becoming one of the first large automotive manufactures to do so. The victory here played a major role in securing landmark Federal labor protection under the Wagner Act and the founding of the UAW in 1935. Closing Auto-Lite's doors in 1962 did not shut out the memories of the tragedy and triumph of 1934."

ACKNOWLEDGMENTS

A heartfelt thank you to Mary and John Whitescarver, Robin Sisak, Denise Russell, Pamela Arendt, John Russell, Lou Hebert, Raymond Blackburn, Judy Sobczak, Marya Sobczak, JoAnn Arendt, Alex Bunshaft, Mike Whitescarver, Brenda O'Donnell, Debbie Pendley, Susanne Junggeburth, Kirsi Hyvärinen, Cindy Bowers, Janice E. Borden, Christina Brauser, Sarah Stamm, Denise Nisbett, Darcy Wilhelm, Michael Brown, Kerri and Joey Lynch, David Russell, Millie Markyvech, Debbie Anderson, Marlo Simmons, Shirley Green, University of Toledo Alumni Association, and Richard Baranowski, local history librarian of Perrysburg Way Library.

Finally, thank you to my husband, Bradley Gayheart. Without his support and encouragement, this book would not be possible.

Several sources were instrumental in my research. Although not all are listed, I would like to give credit to the following:

The Toledo News-Bee (1934)

The Toledo Blade (1934)

New York Times (1934)

Korth, Philip A. and Beegle, Margaret R, *I Remember Like Today: The Auto-Lite Strike of 1934* (Michigan State University Press, 1988)

Lamb, Edward, *No Lamb for Slaughter* (Harcourt, Brace and World, New York 1963)

Dollinger, Sol, *Not Automatic: Women and the Left in the Forging of the Auto Workers' Union* (Monthly Review Press, New York, 2000)

The Literary Digest, *Street Fighting Marks Toledo Strike.* (The Literary Digest, June 2, 1934, Vol. 117, No.22, Whole No. 2302, 1934)

Muste, A.J., *The Battle of Toledo* (The Nation, June 6, 1934, Vol. CXXXVII, No. 3596, 1934)

Muste, A.J., *Heed the Call of Toledo!* (1934). Retrieved from https:// www.marxists. org/ history/ etol/ writers/ muste/ 1935/05/ toledo.htm

Selander, Ted, *A Leader of the 1934 Auto-Lite Strike in Toledo Ohio Tells It Like It Was*, (1986). Retrieved from http:// www.-socialistviewpoint.org/ novdec_06/ novdec_06_06.html

Preis, Art, *Three Strikes that Paved Way for CIO*, (1955). Retrieved from https:// www.themilitant.com/ 1955/ 1922/ MIL1922.pdf

Blount, George and Bailey, Clarence, (1934), *Photo History of the Toledo Auto-Lite strike,* Toledo Lucas County Public Library Digital Collections. Retrieved from https:// ohiomemory.org/ digital/ collection/ p16007coll33/ id/87841/

World Socialist Web Site, *1934 Toledo Auto-Lite strike.* Retrieved from https:// www.youtube.com/ watch?v=qeue-q3AO2v4

Delaney, Nathan D, (2010), *Community Unionism: The Toledo Auto-Lite Strike of 1934.* Retrieved from https:// etd.o-hiolink.edu/ apexprod/ rws_etd/ send_file/ send?accession =Toledo 1271444986 &disposition =inline

AFL-CIO America's unions. Retrieved from https:// aflcio.org

Teamsters History. Retrieved from https:// team-ster.org/ about/ teamster-history/

Zietlow, Rebecca and Pope, James, (2008), The Auto-Lite Strike and the Fight Against Wage Slavery. Retrieved from https:// www.researchgate.net/ publication/ 228128177_ The_ Auto-Lite_ Strike_ and_ the_ Fight_ Against_ Wage_ Slavery

Toledo Lucas County Public Library, *Auto-Lite Strike.* Retrieved from https:// tlcpllaborhistory.omeka.net/ exhibits/ show/ toledo-labor-history/ auto-lite-strike

Lax, Adam, (2008), *"A Rank and File Union Built by the Rank and File" Toledo, Progressives, and the Rise of the UAW 1933-1937*. Retrieved from https:// michiganjournalhistory.files.wordpress.com/ 2014/ 02/ lax.pdf

ABOUT THE AUTHOR

Victoria Arendt was born in Toledo, Ohio. Inspired by travel and movement, she has lived in several different locations, including the vibrant city of San Francisco and the rugged mountains of Montenegro. Currently, she lives in Florida with her husband and scruffy dog named Simon.

www.victoriaarendt.com

ALSO BY VICTORIA ARENDT

Broken Pencils

A NOVEL

In 1934, Ruth, a young housewife, gives birth to a severely handicapped son. Whispers of disgrace and shame swirl in the community as she desperately tries to teach him to be normal. Her embarrassed husband is unsupportive and her mother pressures her to place him into the Insane Asylum. Fearful for his safety, she resists their demands and cares for him at home.

As her son grows and her family expands, feeding, bathing and changing him become increasingly difficult. Reluctantly, she considers the Insane Asylum, until a 1946 Life Magazine article appears, documenting mistreatments, assaults, and massive underfunding of the asylum system.

At sixteen, her son's strength is that of a man and she loses the battle to care for him. He is placed in the Insane Asylum where she witnesses barbaric conditions and inhumane atrocities.

This is the story of Ruth's enormous plight to protect her son from a state system designed to keep *feeble minded imbeciles* incarcerated and away from society. This novel is based on true life events.

Available wherever books are sold.

www.brokenpencilsanovel.com

www.ingramcontent.com/pod-product-compliance
Lightning Source LLC
Chambersburg PA
CBHW030525310726
48979CB00010B/1807/J
* 9 7 8 1 7 3 4 6 3 3 1 8 4 *